# Lost Goat Lane

# Lost Goat Lane

## ROSA JORDAN

Fitzhenry & Whiteside

Text copyright © 2004 by Rosa Jordan
Cover illustration © 2004 by Julie Monk

First published by Fitzhenry & Whiteside in paperback in 2005

First published by Peachtree Publishers in 2004

Published in Canada by Fitzhenry & Whiteside, 195 Allstate Parkway,
Markham, Ontario L3R 4T8

**www.fitzhenry.ca**      **godwit@fitzhenry.ca**

10 9 8 7 6 5 4 3

**Library and Archives Canada Cataloguing in Publication**

Jordan, Rosa
    Lost Goat Lane / Rosa Jordan.

ISBN 1-55041-932-3

    I. Title.

PS8619.O74L68 2005        jC813'.6        C2005-900514-9


Fitzhenry & Whiteside acknowledges with thanks the Canada Council for the
Arts, and the Ontario Arts Council for their support of our publishing program.
We acknowledge the financial support of the Government of Canada through
the Book Publishing Industry Development Program (BPIDP) for our publishing activities.

Book design by Melanie McMahon Ives.
Cover design by Loraine Joyner.

Printed in Canada.

*For my brothers,*
*Alan and Duane*

# Contents

# 1
# Alligators

**K**ate peered through the weeds. Most animals are cute when they're sleeping, but not alligators, she thought. How could anything be cute with such cruddy skin? And those fangy teeth hanging over where their lips ought to be? Though, of course, an alligator doesn't have lips, just a mouth so big you could shove a basketball in it. They also have bad breath, because they swallow their food whole and it lies there in their bellies till it rots. Kate and her brothers, crouched in the high grass on the bank above the big canal, weren't close enough to smell the alligators' breath, but they were close enough to see them clearly. Alligators' legs are so short it's a wonder they can lift their bellies off the ground to run. But they can, and when they do, it's scary how fast they move.

The littlest alligator was about the size of Chip, who was only seven. The middle-sized alligator looked to be five feet long. When Kate turned thirteen at the beginning of the summer, her mom had measured her and that's exactly how tall she was: five feet. Kate often wished she wasn't so skinny, but she'd rather be skinny than shaped like an alligator, fat in the middle and pointy on both ends.

Justin, her big brother, was fourteen. He was taller than Kate. He was skinny like Kate and had long legs. When Justin sprawled out on the couch with his head on the armrest, his feet didn't reach the other end. But the biggest alligator was way bigger than him. If that biggest alligator were to lie down on their couch, he'd hang off both ends.

Justin picked up a rock to throw at the alligators.

"You crazy?" Kate hissed. "You'll wake them up!"

Chip sneezed, and his dog Go-Boy let out a yap. The alligators woke in a flash. The two small ones slid down the bank into the water. But the big one rose up on his stubby legs, ready to charge. He swiveled his big ugly head around and looked at the exact spot where Kate was hiding. Before Go-Boy could let out a second yap, Kate, Justin, and Chip were on their feet, running toward home with Go-Boy in the lead.

Justin quickly passed Kate on the trail and kept going. He was almost around the bend and out of sight when he stopped.

Justin cupped his hands to his mouth and called back to them, "Run! He's right behind you!"

Kate slowed to a walk. She wasn't stupid. If Justin had quit running it was because there wasn't anything to run from.

She turned and called to Chip, "It's okay. There's no gator chasing us."

Chip, still running, looked back over his shoulder. When he did, he stumbled and fell. He hit the ground, *whump!* hard on his stomach. But he didn't cry. One thing you could say for Chip, he didn't cry about every little thing. Kate went back and helped him up.

Justin laughed. "Should have seen your face! You thought that old gator had you by the seat of the pants."

"I wasn't scared," Chip said in a loud voice that told Kate he *had* been scared. "Go-Boy was right behind me. He wouldn't let that gator get near me."

"Ha! Go-Boy'd be no more than a mouthful for a big gator like that."

Chip balled up his fist and punched Justin in the stomach. Justin bent over laughing. "Ow! Ow! You broke my belly."

"I hate you!" Chip said. "I wish you'd disappear."

Justin's laugh stopped like somebody had pushed the off button. "Maybe I will, brat. Someday I will." Justin started up the trail, walking fast.

"It's okay," Kate said to Chip. "He's just..."

She didn't know just what Justin was anymore. He used to be the easiest one in the whole family to get along with, but lately he had changed. He seemed to get mad about something every day.

Kate ran to catch up with him, Chip trailing behind. "What do you mean by that?"

"Just what I said. I could leave anytime."

"Where would you go?"

"Anywhere I please."

Justin was walking so fast that they had to trot to keep up with him.

Chip said, "Mom wouldn't let you. Would she, Kate?"

"She wouldn't even care," Justin retorted.

"She would!" Kate argued. "You know what she says about family sticking together."

"Yeah? Like her and Dad?"

That was a low blow. "It wasn't her fault he never came back," Kate said.

"So whose fault was it? Ours?"

Kate felt sick to her stomach when Justin talked like that. She stopped trying to keep up and let him walk on ahead.

Chip stopped and squatted down to rub Go-Boy's curly head, and the small black dog put out a pink tongue and licked Chip's cheek. Chip stood up and tucked his hand in Kate's. Even though it was sticky-dirty, she held it, because she knew that was something he only did when he felt bad or when he thought she felt bad.

They walked together without saying anything, crossing the highway to a dirt road called Lost Goat Lane. There wasn't a sign or anything like that, but that's what everybody called it. To Kate it seemed like a silly name. As far as she knew, the only goat along the road was her own, and it was in a pen you could barely see from the highway.

Just on the other side of the highway, where the school bus stopped, their own short driveway turned off Lost Goat Lane. It ended in the side yard of their house. It was a small house, just one story built low to the ground, with a front and back porch. There were flower beds all the way around, but most of the flowers had died or gone scraggly because Mom didn't have time to tend them anymore. Two big shade trees in the front yard dropped leaves, which nobody ever bothered to rake. Between the front yard and the highway was a pasture for their three calves and a small drainage ditch. Behind the house were two small sheds. One was for the ducks, and one was for Kate's goat, Sugar.

"Ba-a-a!" the goat bleated as they walked up their driveway. "Ba-a-a!"

Chip looked up at Kate and said, "Sugar's calling you."

Before Kate could answer, Mom hurried out the front door and headed for the car. They could tell by the way she walked, fast without smiling, that she was annoyed. Kate and Chip started to run and got to the car just as she was pulling away.

"How many times do I have to tell you kids I want you home before I leave for work? Do your chores, then get in the house and stay there till I get home," she called out the car window, and drove off without asking where they'd been.

"I don't know why she thinks she's got to remind us to do the chores," Kate grumbled. "How could we forget?"

The calves crowded along the fence making snorty noises at Justin, and the ducks, all quacking at once, waddled toward Chip. Sugar stood on her hind legs against the fence, still saying, "Ba-a-a! Ba-a-a!" Every animal on the place was telling them in its own loud voice that it wanted supper, *now*.

* * *

Kate had just finished milking Sugar and was headed for the back door when she saw the black car coming. The driver was staring at their house. Justin must have seen it, too, because he left the calf pen and walked over to where Kate stood with her pail of milk. Chip came out of the duck shed with a basket of eggs. The three children stood there in a line, with Go-Boy at the end next to Chip, watching the man who was watching them.

The car bounced down the unpaved driveway toward them. It pulled up close—a few more inches and it would have run over their toes. The driver, a thin man with very white skin, the kind you see on people who never go out in the sun, rolled down his window. A cool breath of air-conditioned air floated out.

"Your mother here?" he asked.

"No sir," Kate said. "She's at the dairy where she works."

"I thought she got home at noon."

"She does," Justin said. "But she has to go back at four for the evening milking."

"What day is she off?"

"Cows have to be milked every day. Twice," Justin explained.

"You mean she works every day?" The man said it like there was something wrong with working every day.

"Even birthdays," Chip told him.

"Well, here's my card." The man handed a card to Justin. "Tell her I stopped by."

For a minute the man sat there in his car, looking around. He pointed to the fence that separated their one acre from the surrounding cornfields owned by big farmers.

Kate saw how he pushed his lips together as if he already knew that was the property line.

"Not much to it, is there?" he said.

So what if it wasn't a real farm, just one little acre! she thought angrily. She remembered Dad saying once that the yard might not be much of a yard, but it was big enough for him and his kids to play ball in without hitting one through the neighbor's window. She could have told the man that the little farm was also big enough for goats and calves and ducks, animals that families living in town weren't allowed to have, and she personally would rather have Sugar for a pet than any other animal alive. She also could have told him that when they wanted to build a bonfire to roast hot dogs and marsh-mallows on a summer night, they could do it without the police coming like they did to Mary Ellen's birthday party, and making her parents put it out because night bonfires weren't permitted in city limits.

When nobody answered the man's question, he rolled up his window as if he wanted to keep all the cool air inside for himself, and then drove off.

Kate peered over Justin's shoulder and read the card he was holding. "'Arnold Tate. Bank Appraiser.' What do you suppose he wanted?" she asked. "Why do you think he drove all the way out here?" It seemed like the man could have waited till Mom came into the bank. Something about all this made her worry. Especially when he sat there looking around in that critical way.

Justin looked worried, too, but he didn't answer. He just put the card in his pocket and said, "We better start supper."

Getting supper ready was another chore they had to do every night, and every night it was the same. Kate strained Sugar's milk into a jar and washed out the milk pail. Chip put the duck eggs in their slots in the refrigerator. Justin got some green beans out of the fridge and started snapping them. Kate set the table. Chip climbed up on his step stool at the sink and started washing potatoes for baking.

"I'm sick of taters," Chip complained. "I want some meat."

"Yeah!" Justin said. "How about duck-burgers?"

Chip threw a potato at Justin. It hit Justin in the back, then fell and rolled across the floor. Justin kept on snapping beans like he didn't even feel it. All he said was, "That one's yours."

"Stop teasing him, Justin," Kate said. "Chip, wash off that potato before you put it in the oven."

Chip picked up the potato and flung it on the pan. "I know which one it is, but you don't," he said defiantly, shoving the pan into the oven.

Kate opened the oven door a crack and looked in at the potatoes. Chip was right. There was no way to tell which was the dirty one. "Oh well. Go take your bath, brat."

When Chip finished his bath, Justin took a shower, and then Kate had her bath. After that there was nothing to do but hang around in the living room waiting for Mom to get home.

Chip lay on the floor using his pajama top to play tug-of-war with Go-Boy. Kate tried to read, but lately she had lost interest in the kind of kid books, mostly about animals, that she used to like. But she really wasn't into teenage romances, and the grown-up books she had tried to read didn't hold her attention either. If there were any good ones, she hadn't found them yet. She looked over at Justin. He had one foot up on the sofa and was clipping his toenails. The clipped pieces were flying all over. He wasn't bothering to pick them up.

"Justin, you remember when we went over to Mr. George's house for dinner that time, and afterwards we watched TV?"

"What about it?"

"On TV they showed a man from the bank selling some people's farm."

"Yep," Justin said, and clipped another toenail.

Chip said, "Wish Mom would get our TV fixed."

"Remember, Justin?" Kate said. "The bank took everything."

"What for?" Chip asked.

"Loans," said Justin. "If you don't pay them back, the bank gets everything."

Chip put his arms around Go-Boy's neck. "Everything? Even the animals?"

"Even the kids," Justin said solemnly.

Just then they heard Mom's car pull in.

"You're lying!" Chip yelled. "I'm going to tell Mom!"

"Oh, Chip," Kate moaned. "Can't you take a joke?" She grabbed Chip by the hand and pulled him up off the floor. "Put your pajama top on and help me get supper on the table."

Justin took the potatoes out of the oven and dropped one on each plate, so now even Chip didn't know which was the dirty one. Kate put the green beans in a bowl and poured glasses of goat milk. Chip got a dish of butter and a lump of goat cheese from the fridge and climbed into his chair.

Mom kicked off her muddy boots on the back porch and came into the kitchen in sock feet. She washed her hands at the sink, then sat down at the table and smiled. "Hi, kids," she said in a voice that sounded cheery on the top but tired underneath.

She took a long drink of goat milk. "Mmm, I do love goat milk!" she said. "And goat cheese." She reached for the saucer. "Here, Chip, you want some on your baked potato?"

"I like the yellow kind," Chip mumbled.

Mom stopped pretending to be cheerful. "Goat cheese is what we have, and it's better than store-bought." She plopped a big spoonful on Chip's potato and passed the cheese to Kate.

Kate knew Chip didn't mind goat cheese and milk and potatoes and green beans. But they had that same meal, or something almost like it, so often nowadays that they were all getting sick of it. Mom hardly ever bought groceries anymore. She kept saying they had to get by on what they could raise themselves.

"What did you do today?" Mom asked, trying to sound cheerful again.

"Nothing," Kate said. She didn't look up from her plate.

"Hey, Mom," Chip said. "Dad used to hunt gators, didn't he?"

"Hunting gators is against the law," Mom snapped, her lips tight. "And dangerous. You kids stay away from that big canal, you hear me?"

Kate held her breath. The next question was sure to be, "Have you been hanging around down there?" If they told the truth then they'd get into trouble, and if they lied she would probably find out and they'd get into trouble. Either way, they were doomed. They might get grounded for weeks. To ward off the question she didn't want to answer, Kate said quickly, "A man came this afternoon. From the bank."

Mom sighed.

Justin took the card out of his pocket and laid it by Mom's plate. She barely looked at it.

"What did he want?" Kate asked.

"I'm behind on the payments, that's all. I've asked for an extension on our loan. They have to reappraise the property before they can decide. Chip, stop playing with your food and eat."

Kate thought of how the man had looked at the fence and how disappointed he had seemed that the place was so small. She was pretty sure that he had appraised the property and decided it wasn't worth anything without even bothering to get out of the car.

Mom pushed back her chair and stood up. "That was a nice supper, kids. Now I've got to have a bath."

As soon as Mom left the kitchen, Chip stuck his plate under the table for Go-Boy. The plate came back squeaky clean.

It was Justin's night to wash. He squirted detergent into the dishpan and turned on the hot water. Chip climbed up on the stool beside him to dry.

Kate cleared off the table, then tapped on the bathroom door. "May I come in?"

She knew from the soapy smell coming through the door that Mom would be up to her armpits in a tub filled with bubbles. Kate had given her the bubble bath for her birthday. "Sure," Mom said.

Her eyes were closed. Her long blonde hair was pinned up on top of her head to keep it from getting wet. Kate had seen pictures of Mom when she was a teenager. Her hair was in a ponytail that came halfway down her back. In other grown-up pictures of her, Mom had her hair in long braids wound around her head like a crown. She still fixed it like that sometimes, but mostly she wore it just like it was now, pinned up on her head with bits straggling out all around. Her hair was damp from the steam of the bath water, causing little strands to curl around her face.

Kate tried to remember the last time she saw Mom with her hair fixed up in any particular way. Probably not since Dad left, which was more than three years ago. Thinking about Dad made Kate think about Justin and his talk about going away. Kate squeezed some toothpaste onto her brush. "Mom? How come families don't always stick together?"

"I don't know, honey."

"Do you think some people leave just because they get mad at somebody?"

Mom sighed. "I expect there's more to it than that."

Kate brushed her teeth and rinsed her mouth out.

"Mom? Do you have to work every day?"

"It's that or lose the farm," her mother replied.

"Are we going to?"

"What?"

"Lose the farm?"

"No." Mom wrung out the washcloth and began scrubbing her face, hard.

It was easy to tell when Mom was worried, because with her, the worse things got, the less she said. She used to be a real chatterbox, but after Dad left, and especially when she found out he wasn't coming back, she got quieter and quieter.

At first it hadn't been that bad. Kate sometimes heard her crying at night, but in the daytime her mother was all smiles. "Never mind," Mom had said, making her bright smile even brighter than usual. "We've still got each other." At least once a week she'd taken them to the movies, or roller-skating, or swimming. Mom loved those things as much as they did, and she was great at making up games to play when they were driving somewhere. But that was last year, before she got the job at the dairy. Now, working every single day, she never had time to take them anywhere, or any energy to make up games when they were home.

When school had let out, Kate had asked if they could go camping at the beach this summer. "I'm sorry, sweetie. I can't take the time off work," Mom had said. "And we can't afford it. You kids are going to have to find your own fun this summer."

She did drive them to the shore of Lake Okeechobee on the night of the Fourth of July so they could watch fireworks out over the water, but that wasn't really doing something; it was just watching other people do something. That was why this was turning out to be the most boring summer in history, and why they'd started hanging around the big canal.

***

The very next day Kate, Justin, Chip, and Go-Boy were back at the big canal. This time they were downstream from the alligator lair, under a big shade tree. It was almost too hot to breathe.

"Wish it would rain," Kate said, using the tail of her T-shirt to wipe away the sweat.

"Wish I had some ice cream," Chip said. He lay on his stomach facing Go-Boy. The dog was on his belly with his little black legs stuck out behind. Chip smiled at the dog. "I'd give you some."

Go-Boy wagged his tail as if he understood exactly what Chip said.

Justin said, "If I had money I wouldn't waste it on ice cream."

"What would you buy?" Kate asked.

# Alligators

"A bus ticket." Justin was lying on his back, looking up at the sky. A plane flew overhead, so high it looked like a silver toy. "No, not a bus ticket, a plane ticket," Justin said dreamily. "I'd go to Miami and take a plane."

"Where to?" Kate asked.

"Somewhere where something's happening."

Kate's stomach knotted up the way it always did when Justin talked like that. She used to think that she felt the same, but that was before she understood what Justin really meant. Now when he talked about leaving, he seemed to be thinking about going for good, the way their dad had. She would never want to do that. Her idea of leaving was to go somewhere for a few days, or a week maybe, just for a change.

Camping trips and things like that not only made life more interesting but also gave her something to talk about at school when the other kids were bragging about where they'd been and what they'd done. Kate's favorite place was the beach, which was no more than a two-hour drive. But it might as well be on the moon if you weren't old enough to drive and your mom was working all the time.

"I bet this is the hottest July on record," Kate said.

It was so hot that neither Justin nor Chip bothered to answer. The worst thing about this kind of heat was that it took all your energy. All you felt like doing was lying around. And the more you lay around, the more bored you got. Kate thought of what Mom said about how they had to make their own fun and stretched her mind to think of something.

"I know where some huckleberries are," she said finally, pointing across the canal. "They might be ripe."

"Too far to the bridge," Chip said.

Justin nodded toward the big pipe that ran across the canal. "We could cross there."

Kate snorted. "Nobody in their right mind would try to walk that pipe. What if you fell?"

It wasn't that far from the pipe to the water and all of them could swim. But from where they were sitting they could see the alligators snoozing in the mud. Alligators move fast on land and way faster in the water, especially if they're after something.

"No reason to fall," Justin said. "Anybody could do it."

"You'd be chicken!" Kate scoffed.

*"You're* the chicken," Justin shot back.

"After you!" Kate laughed, knowing he'd never do something that stupid.

Justin got to his feet and strolled down the bank. Kate stopped laughing when he stepped onto the pipe. Hands in his pockets, Justin walked the length of the pipe as casually as if he were on a sidewalk.

He stepped off on the opposite bank and called back, "Now who's chicken?"

"Stay here," Kate said to Chip. She walked down to the canal. Looking upstream, she could see the alligators. They looked like big logs half-buried in the mud. They weren't all that close. They must have gotten used to the kids hanging around and weren't concerned about them anymore. Anyway, they were asleep.

Kate stepped onto the pipe. It was wider than her foot; balancing there wasn't hard at all. She wouldn't think about falling, only about how easy it was.

She walked across, jumped off on the other bank, and gave Justin a shove. "Think you're so smart!"

"How far is it to the huckleberry patch?" he asked.

She was about to answer when they heard Go-Boy barking. Go-Boy wasn't a yappy dog. And this was a nonstop *yap-yap-yap-yap-yap* that said something was seriously wrong. They saw him running back and forth on the opposite bank. Then they saw why. Chip was on the pipe, halfway across the canal.

He stopped and yelled back at the dog, "Stay, Go-Boy!"

Chip made a stay-there motion. He came so close to losing his balance that Kate could almost hear the splash of his body hitting the water. She shuddered. He looked down at the black water below. His face turned pale. Kate knew he was thinking about falling. If he kept thinking about it, it would happen.

"Go back!" Kate yelled.

"Come on!" Justin yelled. "You can make it."

Chip steadied himself and tottered on across, slow at first, and then almost running. Justin held out his hand. Chip grabbed it and leapt to the ground.

"I told you to stay there!" Kate wanted to smack him for scaring them.

Chip stuck out his tongue at Kate, and looked back to make sure Go-Boy had stayed on the other bank. He hadn't. He was in the water, swimming toward them. His little black paws paddled frantically, followed by his curly black head, which barely showed above the water. "Go back, Go-Boy, go back!" Chip screamed.

Go-Boy was a well-trained dog and would do just about anything Chip told him to do. Anything, that is, except stay behind. He kept dog-paddling toward them as fast as he could.

Chip plunged down the bank and straight into the canal. He was up to his waist in the water when Justin caught him.

"Go back, Go-Boy, go back!" Chip screamed again, struggling to get free.

It took Justin and Kate both to drag Chip out of the canal. When they finally got him onto the bank, Justin flung Chip down on the ground and sat on him so he couldn't get away.

By that time they were all soaking wet. Chip stopped screaming and lay there with his face in the mud, sobbing.

Kate looked upstream where the alligators had been sleeping. The two little ones were still there. But the big one was
gone.

"Justin," she whispered. "Look. The big gator..."

They all looked, first for the alligator, then for Go-Boy. They
all saw the same thing. The big gator wasn't there. Go-Boy
wasn't there.

Where Go-Boy had been swimming, they saw only still
black water with a few bubbles coming up to the surface.

# 2

# Goat Love

Chip sobbed all the way home. They practically had to carry him, because he kept stumbling and falling down. Kate saw Mom waiting for them. She would know something was wrong, because Chip never cried unless he was really hurt. Mom came down the porch steps to meet them. "What's the matter?" she asked. "Chip, what is it?

Chip collapsed against Mom's legs and blubbered, "Go-Boy!"

Mom looked Chip over real good. Not seeing blood or anything, she finally turned to Kate and Justin and asked, "Where is Go-Boy?"

When they told Mom that Go-Boy had been eaten by an alligator, a look of horror came over her face. They didn't tell her about how Chip would have drowned himself trying to get to Go-Boy if it hadn't been for them, or how it took about an hour to get him to leave the canal because he kept saying maybe Go-Boy got away. They didn't tell her how they only got him to leave by explaining that when an alligator catches an animal swimming in the water, it holds it under till it drowns, and that those bubbles had been Go-Boy's last breath coming up to the surface. Kate didn't mention how hard it had been to explain all that to Chip when she was crying as hard as he was, and when even Justin had tears running down his cheeks and was so choked up he couldn't talk. Kate didn't try to tell Mom any of that because Mom's face had already gone pale, which in itself was a really scary thing.

Once Mom got the gist of what had happened, she sat down on the steps and pulled Chip into her lap. She held his head against her chest and rocked him while he cried and cried.

Kate would have started crying again herself except that she had already cried herself dry down by the canal. And she knew it wasn't over yet. And she and Justin were probably going to get the worst punishment of their lives for this.

For what seemed like a long time Mom didn't even look at Kate and Justin; she just put her face in Chip's hair and kept rocking him till his sobs quieted down. When she finally did look up at Kate and Justin, there were tears in her eyes and her voice was a whisper. "I thought I could trust you."

It was worse than a punishment.

***

During the next couple of weeks, Mom hardly said a word to Kate and Justin. Justin was as quiet as Mom, and Chip, who had almost always been cheerful, found something to cry about every single day. Kate cried, too, when she was by herself in the milking shed. She kept thinking of Chip tottering on the pipe and Go-Boy paddling over to them. It seemed that as soon as she laid her head against Sugar's soft warm side and started milking, the tears came. Sometimes Sugar looked around from her hay and made a soft *ma-a-a-a*. Kate knew Sugar was trying to make her feel better but it didn't help.

Nothing was going to make her feel better because nothing was going to bring Go-Boy back.

They didn't go to the big canal anymore. They didn't go anywhere. They just hung around the house or the yard waiting till it was time for Mom to get home from the dairy. Only Chip went off by himself sometimes. Once he was gone for a long time. Kate figured he was in the duck shed, sitting in there by himself and crying for Go-Boy.

Sometimes Kate could distract herself with reading and forget for a while what an awful summer this was. But not today, because the book she'd checked out from the library was about some stupid girls chasing some stupid boys. Maybe she'd walk into town in the afternoon and see if she could find a better one. Or maybe she wouldn't. Considering how hot it was and it wasn't even noon yet, she knew that by afternoon it would be too hot to breathe.

Not only was it going to be a scorcher day, it was going to feel like a long one. Usually Mom came home after the morning milking and worked around the house until time to go back for the afternoon milking. But today she had to vaccinate the calves. She wouldn't be getting home from the dairy till after dark.

Kate gave up trying to read and used the paperback book to fan herself. She looked over at Justin, who had stopped sorting through his baseball cards and was staring out the window at Lost Goat Lane, which led to the highway. Kate figured he was thinking about leaving again. Thinking like that was catching, like a cold. As soon as he started getting restless, she started getting restless—not to leave but, well, to do *something*.

If the TV wasn't broken and if Mom hadn't canceled the cable, Justin probably would have been watching a baseball game, because that was his thing. If you had asked Justin whether he'd rather play baseball or breathe, he probably would have said play baseball.

Kate got up and went into the kitchen, but there wasn't anything to do there either—nothing to snack on and no ingredients to make cookies. Kate liked baking. Her mom had even taught her how to make pies. But when they had started running low on money, she said desserts were "non-essentials" and stopped buying chocolate chips and the special stuff you need for baking. There wasn't even enough sugar in the canister to make one batch of cookies.

Kate glanced out the kitchen window and noticed that the gate to Sugar's pen was open. She went out to find the goat and put her back in her pen. She looked behind the goat shed and behind the duck coop, and then walked around the house to the front, where she looked in the calf pasture and in the tall grass by the ditch. Sugar wasn't in any of those places. Neither was Chip. Kate called Chip but got no answer, which made her mad. As small as the farm was, she knew he could hear her calling.

Kate went back to the house and told Justin that Chip and Sugar had disappeared. He was pitching a baseball against the front steps and fielding grounders. He acted like he hadn't heard her.

"Justin!" Kate said loudly. "Did you hear what I said?"

"Yep," he said, throwing the baseball again.

"Well, come on. Help me look for them."

Justin retrieved the ball on the second bounce and stood there for a minute. Then he went inside the house.

Kate found him in the kitchen, drinking a glass of water.

"Justin?" she said again. "Will you please help?

He put down his glass and went back outside, letting the screen door bang in Kate's face.

They walked all the way around the house, looking again in and around the sheds in the back and by the ditch and in the calf pasture out front. They even looked up in the two big shade trees, because Kate was still thinking that Chip was just hiding somewhere, refusing to answer. But there was no sign of him or of Sugar. Then they saw Chip coming up the driveway.

The front of Chip's T-shirt was stained, like he'd been lying in the grass. For a second Kate was reminded of how they'd all crouched in the grass watching the alligators. But Chip had never gone there alone, and she was sure he wouldn't after what happened to Go-Boy. He'd probably gotten the stains from playing by one of the drainage ditches that ran along Lost Goat Lane. He spent a lot of time there catching minnows and looking for turtles. Still, he should've told her and not just wandered off like that.

"Where have you been?" Kate yelled. "And where's Sugar?"

"How do I know?" Chip's eyes were red and his nose was running. "She's your goat."

"Have you seen her?" Kate asked.

"No."

"Then she must've run away," said Justin.

Chip kicked at the dirt with his toes. "I don't care."

Kate hated crying in front of people, especially her big brother, who always teased her. But she couldn't help it. First Go-Boy and now Sugar. She started sobbing.

Justin rolled his eyes. "Jeez, Kate, don't start bawling. Just think like a goat."

Kate wiped her eyes with the back of her hand. "What do you mean?"

"Think what you'd do if you were a goat," Justin repeated.

"Eat," said Chip.

"Look for grass," Kate said.

"So where's the best grass?" Justin asked.

"By the ditches along the road, I guess."

"So let's look there."

They walked to the end of the driveway and looked up and down Lost Goat Lane. In one direction it went only as far as the highway. In the other direction it went so far you couldn't see to the end of it. On both sides of the road were drainage ditches with grassy banks, and beyond the ditches were corn-fields with stalks as high as Justin's head.

"Sugar wouldn't go toward the highway," Kate said. "She's afraid of cars."

"Then she must've gone this way," said Justin. He started walking down the lane, away from the highway. Kate and Chip followed.

"Maybe this is why they call it Lost Goat Lane," Chip said. "'Cause when goats get lost, they come down here."

"Maybe," Justin said. "Used to be lots of goats along here."

"When?" Kate asked.

"Back in the old days, before all the land got bought up by big farmers that live somewhere else." Justin waved his hand at the acres and acres of cornfields on each side of the road. "Used to be quite a few little farms around here. Lots of them had goats, and I guess some of them must've got lost some-time, just like ours."

They came to a crossroad. There was still no sign of Sugar. Justin walked back and forth across the road. "She's been here for sure," he said, pointing to some goat droppings in the dirt.

Just ahead was a house a little bigger than theirs. It had a nice front porch shaded by big trees. There were some sheds out back, and a fenced pasture. It was the farm belonging to the Wilsons. A black family.

# Goat Love

"We going to ask the Wilsons?" Kate asked.

"Might as well," said Justin.

"How come we never go there?" Chip asked.

"No kids," Kate told him. "Anyway, I heard somebody at church say black people would rather be with their own friends."

"Hey, look!" Justin pointed.

On the far side of the Wilsons' pasture was Sugar, standing close to a big, beautiful white billy goat.

When Justin, Kate, and Chip got near the house Kate saw that there were three people on the front porch. The one with gray hair, shelling peas into a pot between her knees, would be Mrs. Wilson. They sort of knew her, because she sometimes walked past their house on her way to town. If they happened to be near the road when she went by, they always said, "Hi, Mrs. Wilson." She always smiled and said "good morning" or "good afternoon" back to them.

Kate had never seen the other two people on the porch. One was a boy about Chip's age, sitting in the porch swing. He held a chapter book, which Kate thought looked too hard for such a little kid. He stopped reading and stared at them.

The other person on the porch was a young woman. She was wearing a halter top, a white miniskirt, and gold thongs. Kate had never seen anybody so beautiful, even in the movies.

"Morning," Kate said to the beautiful woman.

The woman gave a small nod but didn't say anything.

Mrs. Wilson looked up from shelling peas and smiled. "Still morning? Seems like it was getting on to afternoon."

"We lost our goat," Kate explained. She had to do the explaining because Justin was hanging back, as usual. He didn't say much at home, and he hardly ever spoke up around strangers.

"So you did." Mrs. Wilson looked over at the boy on the swing. "Luther, run around the house and tell Grandpa the Martin kids are here for their goat."

The boy called Luther slipped down the steps without looking at them and disappeared around the corner of the house.

Kate couldn't stop staring at the beautiful woman. "I never saw anybody's hair done in little bitty braids with beads all mixed in like that," she said. "It sure is pretty."

"Up in New York where Ruby's been living, lots of folks wear their hair like that," said Mrs. Wilson. "Though I don't know where they find the time. It takes pretty near a whole day to do it up."

The beautiful woman named Ruby still didn't say anything. Kate couldn't think of anything else to say either, so she just stood there in her cutoffs and T-shirt, feeling very unbeautiful.

Luther came back around the house with his grandpa, who they knew was Mr. Wilson. They'd seen him before, too, walking to town with Mrs. Wilson and helping her carry groceries home. Mr. Wilson's hair was pure white and soft looking.

"So that's your nanny goat, is it?" Mr. Wilson asked.

"Yes sir," Kate said. "She's never run away before. Reckon she was looking for some grass."

"Reckon she was looking for a husband," Mr. Wilson said. "And not just any old husband at that. Billy's won first prize at county fair three years in a row."

"We're real sorry if she caused you any trouble," Kate mumbled.

"No trouble," Mr. Wilson said. "But you know it's not free, her keeping company with a pedigreed goat like Billy. Folks pay up to fifty dollars to breed their nannies to my Billy."

Kate understood what Mr. Wilson meant, but couldn't

think of what to say, except the truth. She hesitated a moment, then explained, "We don't have any money. Would you take goat milk for payment?"

Mr. Wilson shook his head. "I got a couple nannies of my own. They give more milk than we can use."

For a minute nobody said anything. Then Chip asked, "How about duck eggs?"

Mr. Wilson looked at Mrs. Wilson, then back at Chip. "Reckon we could use a few duck eggs now and then if you felt like bringing them to us."

"We could do that," Kate said. She was relieved that there was a way they could deal with this themselves, without having to ask Mom for money.

Chip smiled proudly. "Our ducks are real good layers. I gather the eggs every night, and I know."

"That's a good job for a boy your age," Mr. Wilson said. He looked at Kate. "Did you bring a rope to lead your nanny home?"

"No sir."

"Well, maybe I got a little piece," he said, and went into the house.

Ruby, whom Kate had figured out must be the Wilsons' grown-up daughter and also the mother of the boy called Luther, followed Mr. Wilson into the house.

Kate, Justin, and Chip stood at the bottom of the steps waiting for Mr. Wilson to come back with the rope. Mrs. Wilson looked down at them. There were so many turned-up smile wrinkles around Mrs. Wilson's eyes that she always seemed to be smiling, even when she was just shelling peas.

"You got a lot of peas there," Kate said. "You canning?"

"Oh, yes. I put up produce from my garden all summer long. Then my son comes down from Georgia and brings me a big basket of peaches, and I put them up, too." She smiled again. "Your mama still working out at the dairy?"

"Yes ma'am," Kate said. "She usually comes home at noon, but today they're vetting some calves so she won't be back till late."

"Bet you could do with a glass of lemonade before you start home." Without waiting for an answer, Mrs. Wilson started into the house. As she pushed open the screen door, she looked back at them with her crinkly-smiley eyes and asked, "You-all like ham?"

"Yes ma'am!" Chip said.

Mrs. Wilson went inside, letting the screen door close softly.

Luther remained on the porch, watching them from behind a post. Chip looked up at Luther and said, right out of the blue, "I used to have a dog but an old gator ate him."

Luther eased down the porch steps till he was standing face to face with Chip. "All of him?" he asked.

Chip's blue eyes filled up with tears. He looked straight into Luther's brown eyes and said, "Every bite."

Mrs. Wilson came out onto the porch with a plate of sandwiches. Mr. Wilson followed her with a pitcher of lemonade, and Ruby behind them with a tray of glasses. Ruby set the glasses down in a way that made them rattle, like she was mad about something.

"Got plenty of sandwiches here, if you'd care to have one," Mrs. Wilson said.

Chip started up the steps but Kate grabbed him by the shirt and hauled him back. "We're kind of dirty," Kate said. "Can we borrow some water from your hose to wash up?"

"Why sure," Mrs. Wilson smiled. "I'll bring you out a towel." Justin sidled over and joined his brother and sister at the hose. Chip rinsed his hands quickly and ran back to the porch. By the time Kate and Justin got there, Chip was sitting on the swing next to Luther, munching on a ham sandwich.

Everybody had a ham sandwich except Luther. Luther's was peanut butter. "Don't you like ham?" Chip asked.

Luther took a bite of his peanut butter sandwich and thought about it awhile. Then he said, "I do like ham. But I like pigs better. Grandpa's got some pigs. They're real smart."

When they finished eating, Kate offered to help carry things in, but Ruby said, "No need. I've got it." She scooped up everything and went inside, letting the screen slam in a way that let Kate know she didn't want to be followed.

"You just go on around back with Sam and get your goat," Mrs. Wilson said, still smiling.

"Yes ma'am. Thank you for lunch," Kate said, and looked hard at Justin and Chip until they remembered to say thank you, too.

They all told Mrs. Wilson good-bye. Then Justin said, "Come on, Chip," and headed for the road. Kate knew that was Justin's way of saying it was her responsibility to go get Sugar, since Sugar was her goat. So Kate followed Mr. Wilson around back to the goat pen.

"Long about five months from now," he said as he tied the rope around Sugar's neck, "this little nanny's going to have a nice surprise for you."

Kate had lived on a farm long enough to know exactly what kind of surprise he was talking about. "Thanks, Mr. Wilson," Kate said. "We sure do appreciate it." Mostly what she appreciated was the fact that Mr. Wilson didn't say any more about how much it cost to breed a nanny to his prize-winning billy. He just handed the lead rope to Kate, said "There you are, girl," and went back into the house.

Sugar was not enthusiastic about leaving Billy. She kept trying to go toward the pasture instead of the road. Kate had to drag her, which was hard because Sugar weighed at least as much as Kate. Kate stopped to rest in the shade of the house, hoping that Justin would wonder what was taking so long and come help her.

That's when she heard Ruby's voice coming through the kitchen window. "You ought to be ashamed of yourself, Papa, taking eggs off such raggedy-assed kids."

"Mind your language there, girl," Mr. Wilson scolded. "I don't reckon a few eggs are going to hurt anybody. What we're needing is not eggs so much as some children for that boy of yours to play with."

"I told you, Papa. I don't want Luther hanging around with white trash!"

Kate's face burned as if it had been slapped. Part of her wanted to run away. The other part of her wanted to stomp that beautiful woman right on her beautiful painted toenails. For a minute Kate just stood there, too angry to move, almost too angry to breathe.

Then she heard Mrs. Wilson's voice. "Being poor don't make them trash, Ruby. There's not a soul in this county works as hard as their mother. Don't you remember? I wrote you a while back that Mr. Martin had gone off and left them."

"That's not my problem," Ruby snapped.

"I'm surprised at you," Mrs. Wilson said in a sorrowful voice. "You know yourself how hard it is for a woman to raise a child all by herself. Mrs. Martin's got three to look after."

Sugar tugged at the rope again, trying to get back to Billy. Kate realized that if Sugar let out one *ba-a-a* they'd look out the window and see her and think she was eavesdropping. She gave the rope a sharp yank and walked quickly away from the house. As they neared the road Sugar started walking normally, apparently having decided that she didn't mind going home after all. Chip and Justin had already started walking back.

"Justin!" Kate called. "Wait."

Justin and Chip waited until she caught up to them.

"I don't think we ought to—" Kate was going to say she didn't think they ought to come here again, but changed her mind. If she said that, they'd ask why, and if she told Justin and Chip what she'd heard, they'd feel just as bad as she did. What was the point?

"I know what you were going to say," Chip said. "You don't think we ought to tell Mom."

Justin and Kate looked at each other. She knew what he was thinking, and he probably knew what she was thinking. Mom already didn't trust them, and now that they'd let Sugar get out, she was going to trust them even less.

"We'll tell her," said Kate. "But not just yet, okay?"

Sooner or later they would tell Mom. They'd have to, because in about five months, probably around Christmas, Sugar was going to have a baby.

# 3
# Turtles and Trophies

The following week, Justin, Kate, and Chip walked down Lost Goat Lane to the Wilsons' to take the duck eggs. Kate carried the bag of eggs because Justin, as usual, was busy pitching a baseball in the air. Chip held two small turtles, one in each hand.

Luther saw them coming and ran up the road to meet them.

"Where'd you buy them?" Luther asked, staring at the two turtles.

"You don't buy them," Chip said. "You just find them."

"Where?"

"On the road. Or in the ditch. They're all over. This kind and snapping turtles, too." Chip handed one of the turtles to Luther. "Don't hold it up close. It might wet on you."

The minute Luther took the turtle, it let loose a stream of urine. Luther giggled and held the turtle away from him.

"You want it?" Chip asked. "You can have it."

"Sure!" Luther said. "What's his name?"

"Hasn't got one yet. I just found it on the way up here."

"I'm going to call him Mr. P.," Luther said. Both boys laughed so hard they nearly fell down.

"You can have this one, too," Chip said. "So they can keep

each other company. You got some chicken wire to make them a pen? They don't like living in little bitty boxes."

"Grandpa's got some wire," Luther said, "in his work-shop."

As soon as they reached the house, Luther and Chip disap-peared around back in the direction of Mr. Wilson's workshop. Justin followed them. Kate went up on the porch and knocked on the screen door.

Ruby came to the door.

"Here's your eggs," Kate said.

Ruby opened the door a crack and took the bag.

"I'll tell Papa you brought them," Ruby said, and let the screen slam shut in Kate's face.

Kate stood on the porch for a minute, not knowing what to do. Should she go around back and look for Chip and Justin, or just go home? While she was trying to decide, Mrs. Wilson came out on the porch.

"Long as you're here, Kate, wonder if you'd give me a hand in the garden? My back doesn't bend as good as it used to."

"Yes ma'am." Kate didn't care much for garden work, but it was better than not knowing what to do.

They passed a tin-roofed shed in the backyard. Half of it was a goat shed that opened into the pasture. The other half opened into the yard and served as Mr. Wilson's workshop. It had only one wall, in the back, to separate the goats' part of the shed from the workshop part. The workshop didn't have walls on three sides, so what little breeze there was passed through and kept it cool. Something that looked like a large wooden crate sat on the workbench. Mr. Wilson and Justin were helping Chip and Luther unroll and measure a length of wire for the turtle pen. Kate followed Mrs. Wilson to the gar-den. Mrs. Wilson set the basket down between two rows.

"This yellow squash is coming on so fast I can't keep up with it," she said. "You take that row and I'll take this one, and we'll scoot the basket along between us."

Kate knelt down at the end of the row and started picking the yellow crookneck squash. "Your garden's bigger than ours." Kate glanced across the yard at the flower beds that went all the way around the house. "And you got real pretty flowers."

"I couldn't do without my flowers," Mrs. Wilson said, her dark brown fingers searching among the big green squash leaves and snapping off the little yellow crooknecks. "Back when I was a girl, a lady at church showed us flower arranging, that's what got me started. Ruby, now, she's got an artistic streak, too, but she'd rather work with store-bought stuff. Not me. When I get the itch to be creative, I want to lay my hands on something natural."

"We used to have flower gardens around the house, but Mom doesn't have time anymore," Kate told her.

Mrs. Wilson tilted her head to one side, and her eyes got a remembering look in them. "I didn't either when I was working. Saving up to buy this farm, Sam and me worked two jobs apiece. Then the children came along." She smiled over the top of the squash leaves at Kate. "But there's a secret folks don't tell young'uns about getting older."

"What?" Kate asked.

"When a person starts getting up in years, they get to do more and more just what they want to do. Why, when I was young, I was so busy trying to please teachers and preachers and parents and brothers and sisters and my husband and my children, I had no time to think about what I'd rather be doing." Mrs. Wilson's voice dropped low and confidential. "But now, sometimes I don't even go to church. Me and the

Lord spend many a Sunday morning all by ourselves out amongst the flowers."

Mrs. Wilson glanced at the basket of squash, which was about as full as it could get. "That ought to do," she told Kate. "With Ruby and Luther here there's lots more cooking than when it was just Sam and me. But I'm not complaining. I'm just glad she came home. It was real hard, her trying to work and look after Luther all by herself in the city."

"Are they going to stay?" Kate asked.

"Well now, it's hard to tell." Mrs. Wilson stared off into the distance, like she was trying to see into the future. "Ruby's a restless one. From since she was a little girl, she was always wanting to go somewhere. That's how come she was up in New York when Luther was born. She liked it okay up there, liked working in that fancy candy shop. But then she got laid off. She couldn't find another job that would support her and Luther both. So she came on back, which to my way of thinking is a good thing. The way families spread out now makes it harder on everybody. But 'specially the little ones."

Kate picked up the basket of squash. Mrs. Wilson got up and walked alongside her, headed toward the house. Kate was thinking about when her dad left. It had probably been hardest on Mom because now she had to do all the work and worrying about how to make ends meet. If Justin left, Mom would really freak. "Justin's getting restless like that," she said. "Even our animals act like they don't like living at home anymore. The ducks are always hiding their nests and the calves keep getting out, and then Sugar ran away. She never did that before."

Mrs. Wilson smiled at Kate. "Seems to me like your nanny wasn't running away from you all. She was just going down the road a ways to find her some more family. When those little ones are born, she'll want to be right there in her own pen."

"You think she'll have more than one?" Kate asked in surprise.

"Well now, she might. Billy's got a habit of fathering twins."

The back of the Wilsons' house was just like theirs: it had a screen door that led onto a back porch, and another door into the kitchen. But when Kate followed Mrs. Wilson inside, she felt like she'd entered a foreign country.

Music was playing at top volume. Ruby, with a broom in her hand, was dancing around the room. Long black braids swirled around her shoulders, and a short skirt swirled around her thighs. She might be stuck-up, but no doubt about it, she really grabbed your attention.

"Ruby!" Mrs. Wilson shouted. "Can you turn it down a little?"

Ruby stalked over to the radio and turned it down.

"I like that music," Kate said shyly. "Is that New York music?"

Ruby rolled her eyes at Kate. "Heavens, girl. You never heard reggae before?"

"Our TV broke," Kate explained, feeling incredibly stupid. "And Justin's always got the radio tuned to a ball game."

"Well, for your information, reggae didn't start in New York. Comes from the Caribbean. Jamaica and places like that. The best reggae bands all come from there."

Ruby danced her way from the kitchen into the living room. Kate could tell that Ruby wasn't interested in talking to her. But she was about the most exotic person Kate had ever seen up close. Using another question as an excuse, she followed her into the living room. "Do they do that kind of dancing in Jamaica?"

"What?" Ruby looked around like she was surprised Kate was still there. "Oh, I don't know. Never been to Jamaica. But someday I'm going."

Just then Kate caught sight of a U.S. map tacked to the wall over a desk in the corner. "Is it far?" Kate asked. "Where is it?" She didn't really care where it was, but she knew that the best way to get an adult to talk to you was to ask questions.

Ruby clicked her tongue as if to say she'd never met a person so ignorant, but Kate could tell that she liked being the one with all the answers.

"Not all that far." Ruby pointed a plum-colored fingernail at the map. "We're here in south Florida. Cuba's this next island, and that one's Jamaica. It wouldn't take more than a day to get there by car. Except Jamaica's out in the ocean so you couldn't get there in a car. Have to take a boat. Or a plane."

"I've never flown in a plane," said Kate. "Have you?"

"Sure." Ruby flopped down on the couch in a way that made her look limp and restless at the same time. "Luther and me flew down here from New York just this summer."

Kate looked around the living room. It was almost like theirs, but not exactly. There were magazines, and a knitting basket, and a vase with fresh flowers. It was the kind of stuff they used to have, but Mom didn't have time for anymore. Kate was trying to think of a question to ask Ruby about New York when the screen door crashed open and Luther and Chip burst into the room. They were laughing in that silly way little boys do when there's nothing at all to laugh about.

Ruby's eyes flashed angrily, and Kate remembered what she'd said about not wanting Luther to play with "white trash."

"We gotta go," Kate said quickly, and reached for Chip's hand.

Chip snatched his hand away and glared at Kate as if she was being mean.

Kate felt mean. This was the first time she'd seen Chip

having fun since the alligator ate Go-Boy. And now she had to spoil it.

Chip gave Kate a stubborn look, like he was going to put up a fuss. But Chip often had a way of figuring out what was going on even when nobody explained it to him, and Kate saw that he had figured out this situation, too. Without anybody saying anything, he seemed to understand that playing with Luther wasn't up to Kate. He walked over to where Ruby was sitting on the couch and looked straight into her eyes.

"Can I come back tomorrow?" he asked. "Luther's grandpa is going to help us build a pen for the turtles."

Ruby's pretty mouth was pinched shut the way mothers' mouths always are when they don't approve of something. Luther came to stand beside Chip. "Please, Mama?"

Ruby put her hand on top of his curly black hair. The corners of her lips softened. She didn't smile, but almost. Kate could tell that whatever Luther wanted, Ruby wanted him to have. Ruby looked at Chip and sighed. "You want to come over now and then, I guess that's okay."

The screen door banged again. It was Mr. Wilson and Justin. "Care to sit a spell, Justin?" Mr. Wilson motioned to the couch.

"I think we better be getting home," Justin said. But as the words came out of his mouth, something seemed to work on Justin like a magnet, pulling him into the room.

Kate looked to see what it was. It was a shelf filled with baseball trophies. Justin moved closer to them. In a low, surprised voice, he read, "Booker Wilson. Booker Wilson. Booker Wilson."

"That's my boy," Mr. Wilson said proudly.

"My dad used to say Booker Wilson was the best ballplayer this town ever produced," Justin said.

Kate didn't remember back to when Booker still lived in town. Justin probably didn't either, which is why he was just now putting Booker Wilson the ballplayer together with this Wilson family.

Mr. Wilson sat down in a rocking chair and looked up at all the shining trophies. "Yep, a fine ballplayer. He had a notion he could make it to the majors, but after a couple years in the minors, well, he decided to go in the army to get himself some more education."

"I sure would like to see him play!" Justin said, his eyes shining. "Where is he now?"

"Coaching up in Atlanta." Mr. Wilson rocked slowly in his chair. "He always comes home for Thanksgiving. You-all want to meet him, why, come on by."

Kate shot a look at Justin's face. From the way he was grinning, you'd have thought Mr. Wilson had just handed him a ticket to the World Series.

# 4
# The Worst School Year

We sure had a time of it vaccinating all those calves," Mom said at supper. "What did you all do today?"

"Nothing," said Justin.

"Mom," Kate said quickly, to change the subject, "when we go shopping for school stuff can I get a skirt and—"

"A skirt wouldn't be practical. If I had the money for anything, it would be new sneakers and jeans. But I'm afraid we won't be doing any shopping for school."

"No shopping?" Justin looked surprised.

"But, Mom!" Kate said. "School starts in two weeks!"

"I know when school starts," said Mom.

"I need a Ninja notebook!" said Chip.

"Buy me some fabric then," Kate pleaded. "I'll make one." It occurred to Kate that fabric would be even better because she could make the skirt as short as she liked. Once the skirt was cut out, Mom couldn't make her make it longer and wouldn't want the material to be wasted. Kate could end up with a skirt as short and swingy as Ruby's.

Mom didn't answer. Suddenly Kate started getting scared. Every year since first grade they had gone shopping for clothes and classroom supplies a week or two before school started. How could they start a new school year without buying the stuff they needed? They all stared at Mom. Mom stared at her plate.

"We don't have any money. Not even enough for new shoes." Mom's voice dropped to a whisper. "I'm sorry."

Justin got up from the table and carried his plate over to the sink. It was still half-full of food. He scraped it into the compost and started to run the dishwater.

"Justin?" Mom said. "You didn't eat—"

"I'm done," Justin said. He didn't raise his voice, but Kate could tell he was mad. He dumped way too much detergent in the dishpan and turned the water on full blast. Soapsuds splashed up on the counter.

"Does this mean I have to use last year's notebook?" Chip asked, looking like he was going to cry.

"I'm afraid so. For now, anyway." Mom sounded miserable.

"Maybe I could get a job," Kate said. "You know, after school."

Mom's eyes filled up with tears. "Oh, Katie, you're such a good girl. But no, honey, I don't want you going out to work. Anyway, I need you to be here to look after Chip."

Mom got up and went into the bathroom. Kate started to follow her, to tell her that she just could not wear last year's school clothes. Kate was still skinny, but her jeans, shirts, and T-shirts, most of which had been new last school year, were getting so tight in some places that it was embarrassing to wear them.

Kate lifted her hand to knock, then changed her mind. She could hear muffled sounds through the bathroom door. Mom was crying.

\*\*\*

As Kate waited for the school bus with Justin and Chip, she knew this was going to be the worst first day of school of her life. Everybody noticed what everyone else was wearing on the first day of school, more than any other time. Kate's shirt was so tight across the chest that she was afraid to take a deep breath. Her sneakers, like Chip's and Justin's, had holes in them and were worn down at the heels.

Kate tugged at her shirt, which she couldn't tuck in because her jeans were already too tight. "They're going to make fun of me," she said miserably.

"Who cares?" Justin stared at the ground as if he hated the dirt. "If Mom can't buy school clothes she sure can't make mortgage payments. That means we're probably going to lose the farm, which means we'll probably be moving anyway."

Kate had almost forgotten about Mom being behind on the mortgage payments. She had considered what might happen to the animals if they lost the farm, but maybe because this was the only place she'd ever lived, she hadn't pictured the whole family actually moving someplace else. Why did Justin have to bring it up now?

"Here they come!" shouted Chip.

Ruby was heading up Lost Goat Lane with Luther. She wore matching jeans and jeans jacket. The silver buckle on her belt flashed in the sun as she walked. Kate thought she looked like somebody you'd see on TV. And Luther looked like a boy in a commercial for kids' clothes. Everything he had on was brand-new. His sneakers were pure white. But the way he was hanging onto his mother's hand showed that he was scared.

"Luther!" Chip yelled. "Hurry! The bus is coming!"

Suddenly Luther lost his scared look. With a happy smile, he let go of his mother's hand and ran to meet Chip.

The bus stopped and the door swung open. Chip and

Luther clambered up the bus steps together. Justin followed them.

Kate looked up at the kids looking out the bus window at her. Somebody laughed, and she heard the word "floods." That's what they called pants that were too short.

Kate bowed her head and climbed onto the bus. The worst summer of her life had ended. She was pretty sure this was the start of the worst school year of her life.

***

Kate was right. Every day from the time she got on the bus in the morning till she got home in the afternoon the other kids teased her. Each time it was something different. One day the middle button popped off her shirt and she had to fasten it shut with a safety pin. The pin was bad enough, but while Kate was taking a test and not paying attention, Schroder, the boy who sat behind her, stuck a note on her back.

When she walked up to the teacher's desk to hand in her test, the whole class saw it and started laughing. When Kate realized they were laughing at something on her back, she reached over her shoulder and pulled it off. It said, "Kate's tits are too big for her shirt." Kate's face burned. The truth was that they weren't too big; they only stuck out about an inch. The shirt was just too small. The last thing she wanted was for the whole school to be cracking jokes about her body, especially that part of her body.

She knew Schroder was the one who put it there. He was the smallest boy in the class, with a short blond crew cut and baby blue eyes. He was always in trouble, usually for using bad language. He had no fear of teachers and would do anything for a laugh.

The teacher, Mrs. Morton, took the note out of Kate's hand, glanced at it, and dropped it into her pocket. "Schroder," she said, "I want you to stay after class."

"Who, me?" Schroder asked, his blue eyes opened wide with fake surprise. "What for, Mrs. Morton?"

The class laughed even harder, especially the boys. "That's enough now," Mrs. Morton said. She looked at her watch. "Those of you who haven't turned in your paper yet have just five more minutes." Before the class ended, the teacher added, "On second thought, I want *all* the boys to stay after class."

The bell rang and the girls raced down the hall to the cafeteria. Kate followed slowly. She didn't feel like facing them. She stood in the hallway a minute, then ducked into the bathroom. A toilet stall was about the only place in the whole school where you could have any privacy.

\*\*\*

That night, when she was washing dishes and Justin was drying, he asked, "How come you didn't go to lunch today?"

Kate was surprised by the question. Their school had a big cafeteria. Kate normally sat on one side with grade seven students. Justin sat on the other side with the grade nines, with the grade eight students in between. Sometimes she caught a glimpse of Justin, but he never seemed to notice her. He hardly ever spoke to her at school, even if they passed in the hall.

Too embarrassed to tell Justin about what happened, Kate tried to think up some excuse for missing lunch. Before she could answer, Justin spoke up again.

"I heard Morton made the boys stay after class," he said, "for a lecture on sexual harassment."

Kate knew it was Brad Anderson who had told Justin. Brad was in Kate's class. Normally a ninth grader wouldn't be

42

caught dead hanging around with a seventh grader, but it just happened that Brad was a super pitcher. Almost every day after lunch Justin borrowed a glove and played catch with Brad because it was a well-known fact that if you could catch Brad's throws, you could catch anybody's. Kate figured Brad had told Justin about Schroder putting the note on her back, plus whatever Mrs. Morton said to the boys. She was wondering exactly what Mrs. Morton had told them, when Justin snickered.

"What's so funny?" Kate asked sharply. "What did Brad say?"

"He said Morton gave them a lecture on sexual harassment. She wrote T-E-A-T-S on the board and told them it was a word that should only be used for animals that give milk. Schroder asked her what word they should use for humans and she said there was no need to use any word because whatever they think about girls' bodies, they ought to keep to themselves."

"Yeah!" Kate said. She was surprised that Mrs. Morton had stuck up for the girls like that. Mrs. Morton was the kind of teacher who never yelled, but never smiled either. Once when the girls got to giggling about something and wouldn't settle down, Mrs. Morton had sighed and said she understood why some teachers preferred to work in an all-boys' school. Kate had taken that to mean that her teacher liked boys better than girls. But maybe she hadn't meant it like that. Maybe when Mrs. Morton had to deal with boys like Schroder, she felt like going to teach in an all-*girls'* school.

"What is sexual harassment, exactly?"

The way Justin always seemed to be off in his own world with nothing on his mind but baseball, you wouldn't expect him to be the kind of brother you could ask for information, but Kate knew she could, and trusted his answers. Mom, of course, had explained to her all the girl stuff about her body, but since they were little, she'd ask Justin about things, and if he didn't know, he'd ask Dad. That's how they found out everything. Now Dad wasn't around to ask, but Justin was still the best source of information for anything related to school.

Justin stood there for a minute flipping the dish towel. He used to drive Kate crazy snapping it at her behind, but he didn't do that anymore. "Bugging girls about their bodies," he finally answered. "Like what Schroder did." Justin gave the towel a couple more snaps, then said in a puzzled voice, "I thought it was just doing mean things. But Brad said Morton told them compliments can be harassment, too."

\*\*\*

Kate didn't know if she'd feel harassed by compliments or not, because she never got any. All she got at school was mean teasing, and not always from the boys. In fact, the girls were worse. They competed with each other to see who could say the most hateful things about her clothes. One day during a softball game, Kate made a good long hit and took off on what she knew would be a home run. But the lace in one sneaker broke, and as she rounded second base, the shoe went flying into the air. The girl on second base caught the shoe and threw it to home. The catcher caught it, touched the plate, and yelled, "Out! Ragfoot's out!" Kate tried to get the shoe back, but they kept throwing it from one to another, yelling, "Out, Ragfoot! You're out!"

Finally Kate went into the girls' restroom and locked herself in a toilet stall. It wasn't that she liked it in there, but where else could she go? The only other private place was the nurse's office, and you really had to be sick, with a fever or bleeding or something, before you'd be allowed to lie down in there—and then just to wait till your mother came for you.

Kate had been in the stall a few minutes when the bell rang. A minute later, a bunch of girls ran giggling into the bathroom. One of them threw the shoe over the top of the stall. Kate put it back on, but she didn't go to class. The giggling trickled out the door and it got quiet. Then someone else came into the bathroom. The second Kate saw the person's feet, she knew it was Miss Lynn, the librarian. Miss Lynn always wore shoes that looked like slippers. They were made of cloth or soft leather, and had fancy designs on the toes. If she saw you looking at them, she would tell you all about the girls in China or the Indian women in Ecuador who made them. Miss Lynn traveled every summer, and she must have spent most of her time shopping for shoes, because she had slipper-shoes from just about every place you could think of.

Miss Lynn's feet stopped in front of Kate's toilet stall.

"Kate?" Miss Lynn called softly. "Are you okay?"

For a second Kate couldn't figure out how Miss Lynn knew who was in the toilet stall. Then she realized that Miss Lynn must have seen her shoes under the stall door, too. She had recognized Miss Lynn by her pretty slippers. Miss Lynn had recognized her by her ragged tennis shoes. Kate felt her face flush hot with embarrassment.

"I've got a stomachache," Kate muttered.

"Do you want me to call your mother to come get you?"

"She's at work," Kate lied. In fact, Mom came home at noon and didn't go back to work until four, so she was almost certainly at home right now. But the last thing Kate wanted to do was to tell Mom what had happened. If she had any money to buy them new shoes, she would have done it already. If she didn't have the money, telling her about the mean teasing would just make her feel bad.

"Is there a phone where she works?" Miss Lynn asked.

"Not in the dairy barn," Kate said. She wished Miss Lynn would go away and mind her own business.

But Miss Lynn kept standing there, close to the stall door, where Kate could see her shoes. Today she was wearing fringed leather slippers with tiny beads sewn in a design on the toes.

"You can't spend the afternoon in here," Miss Lynn said firmly.

Kate didn't answer.

"What class do you have this period?"

"Study hall," Kate mumbled.

For a minute Miss Lynn just stood there, tapping one moccasined foot on the tile floor. Finally she said, "I don't have a class this period. If you just need some quiet time, you can come into the library."

Kate came out of the toilet stall. She didn't look at Miss Lynn, but walked beside her down to the library.

"I like your shoes," Kate said. It was her way of thanking Miss Lynn, because she knew Miss Lynn liked it when people admired her shoes.

"This is my favorite pair," Miss Lynn said. "They were made by Navajo Indians in Arizona."

When they got to the library, Miss Lynn gave Kate a book that showed how the Navajo people made designs on clothes with tiny beads. Kate flipped through the book for a few minutes just to please Miss Lynn, not actually reading it but looking at the pictures, which weren't that interesting. She put her head down on the table and wished it was time to go home.

Miss Lynn noticed that she had stopped reading the Indian beading book and brought her another one called *West with the Night*.

"What's it about?" Kate asked. She usually didn't like the books grown-ups picked for her.

"It's a true story," Miss Lynn said, "about an English girl who grew up in Africa. She used to go hunting with the natives and once got attacked by a lion. When she was a teenager she became a racehorse trainer, and then she learned to fly planes. She was the first woman to fly alone across the Atlantic Ocean."

Miss Lynn went back to her desk, but kept glancing at Kate. Kate figured that if she didn't want to get sent to study hall, she'd better at least pretend to be reading. She skimmed the first chapter, which was about flying a plane somewhere to rescue a dying man. As she expected, it was not very interesting. But it got better in the next part, where the little girl sneaks away from school and goes with the Africans who live on her father's farm to hunt wild pigs with spears. Kate had just gotten to the paragraph where a wild pig gored the girl's dog when the bell rang. Since it was a true story, she figured the dog would die. She left without asking to check out the book.

But when the mean teasing started at lunch the next day, she went to the library and asked Miss Lynn if she could come there in the afternoon and read instead of going to P.E. and study hall. Miss Lynn said she would have to talk to Kate's teachers. When Kate came back the next day, Miss Lynn said Kate would have to go to P.E., but she could spend study hall period in the library—as long as she was reading or doing schoolwork.

Kate suspected that Miss Lynn or the gym teacher must've had a talk with the girls in her P.E. class, because nobody said anything mean to her. They just treated her like she was invisible. Which was okay, she told herself, because at the end of the period she *would* disappear, into the library. After a few days, a couple of girls asked why she didn't come to study hall anymore, but she just shrugged and didn't answer. She liked it that they didn't know.

In the library Kate usually got at least a start on her homework, which she had hardly ever managed to do in study hall. It was hard to work in there with the kids whispering and passing notes and throwing spitballs and being yelled at by the teacher, who wasn't very good at keeping order. She never got her homework finished, though, because after P.E., especially on hot days, the quiet of the library made her sleepy. As long as Kate was working, Miss Lynn didn't leave her desk. But the minute Kate started staring out the window or put her head down on the table, the librarian would bring her another book. The next book Miss Lynn gave her was called *Road Song*.

When Kate asked what it was about, Miss Lynn said, "It's about a little girl who gets attacked by a team of sled dogs and gets one side of her face eaten off."

Kate almost gagged. It didn't help when Miss Lynn added, "It's a true story."

But with Miss Lynn looking up from her desk every couple of minutes to see if she was reading, Kate didn't have much choice. *Road Song* had been written by the girl who got half her face bitten off. It turned out to be a good book, only a little bit gruesome, and not at all depressing. Like most grown-up books, it started off boring, but by the second chapter, she forgot all about Miss Lynn and the library. Even the gruesome parts were better than study hall, with the girls whispering, probably about her, and boys bouncing spitballs off the back of her head.

# 5
# Almost a Friend

Kate would have been perfectly happy to go home in the afternoon and keep reading about interesting people in faraway places. The problem was that they got home from school just as Mom was leaving for work, and Kate's first chore was to help Chip with his homework. Justin could have done it, but he got too impatient. Sometimes Kate couldn't explain things either, at least not in a way her little brother could understand. Chip had the most trouble with arithmetic, which wasn't Kate's best subject. One day she had an idea. Chip and Luther were in the same class. Mrs. Wilson or Ruby was probably helping Luther. Maybe they could help Chip, too.

"Come on, Chip," Kate said. "Let's go down and see how Luther's doing with his homework."

When they came up onto the Wilsons' porch they saw Luther through the screen door. He was sitting at the desk under the big U.S. map. Ruby was standing beside him.

When Kate knocked, Ruby looked up and said sharply, "Luther can't play. He's got homework."

"So does Chip," Kate said through the screen. "I explained borrowing about ten times and he's still getting it wrong. I was wondering if you—"

"Hey, Chip," Luther interrupted. "Did you get number three?"

Chip pushed open the screen door. Kate grabbed at the tail of his T-shirt to stop him from walking right in, but he pulled away from her and went straight over to the desk. He looked at Luther's paper and said, "Three was easy. It's number five, with all the zeros."

"Oh, I can show you zeros," Luther said. He slid out of his chair. "Let's go in on the kitchen table."

Luther led Chip out of the room and Kate followed them. Behind her, she heard Ruby sigh.

"Grandma," said Luther, "will you help us?"

"Reckon I can cook and do arithmetic at the same time," Mrs. Wilson said. All the wrinkles at the corners of her eyes crinkled into a smile. She looked at Kate over the boys' heads. "I could when Ruby was a little girl."

"Thanks, Mrs. Wilson." Kate gave Mrs. Wilson a grateful smile. "I think I'll wait in the living room if that's okay."

"You do that, honey. The boys and me will do just fine."

Chip and Luther put their books on the kitchen table. Kate slipped back into the living room and stood there waiting for Ruby to say, "Have a seat." But Ruby didn't say anything.

Kate stood next to the desk, feeling awkward. There was an electric typewriter on the desk. Kate touched it. "Wish I could type," she said.

"What for?" asked Ruby. "That's old technology."

"I know. But Miss Lynn said that people who know how to touch type get their work done way faster, even when they're using the computer," Kate said. She hesitated and added, "I like knowing how to do things. It makes me feel like I'm smarter than folks think I am."

Kate could have explained to Ruby that when you're pretty

or have cute clothes it doesn't matter if you're smart because people notice you no matter what. But when you're just an ordinary-looking person you have to be smart or else they treat you like you're invisible, and only notice you if they're feeling mean and need somebody to pick on. But Kate didn't try to explain this because she figured it wasn't the sort of thing Ruby would understand. She just stood there with her fingers on the typewriter keys, wishing she could do something that would make Ruby notice her.

Ruby flopped down on the couch and started flipping through a magazine. Suddenly she lowered the magazine and looked at Kate's hands. "I never saw such filthy fingernails! What have you been doing?"

Kate had never paid much attention to her own fingernails. She looked down at them now and pulled them away from the typewriter keys. "Uh, I don't know," she said, curling them into the palms of her hands.

Ruby got up and went down the hall. A minute later she came back with a manicure set. "Sit," she said, pointing to a chair.

Kate perched on the chair. Ruby sat on the couch across from her. She took one of Kate's hands into her lap and started cleaning the dirt out from under the fingernails. Kate felt uneasy having Ruby work on her nails. She could tell Ruby was only doing it because she was bored, or maybe because she thought Kate wasn't well-groomed enough to be hanging around their house. Kate couldn't stop thinking about Ruby's remark about "white trash." She tried to think of something to say that would interest Ruby and get her mind on something besides all the dirt under her fingernails.

"Can I ask you a question?" Kate asked.

"Ask away," Ruby said.

"What I wonder," Kate said, "is why, at school, white kids and black kids and Latinos and Asians hang out mostly with other kids like them. Not all the time, of course, but most of the time, like in the lunchroom, or after school." Kate waited a moment, then asked the rest of her question. "You think it's because everybody's prejudiced against everybody else?"

Ruby kept working on Kate's fingernails. Instead of answering, she asked, "Who do you hang out with, Kate?"

Kate felt her face turning red. "Nobody, really. I had a good friend in fifth grade, but she moved away."

Ruby started filing the rough edges off Kate's nails. "But if you had a choice, who would it be? Somebody just like you, right?"

Kate heard the suspicious tone in Ruby's voice and understood what she was getting at. She answered carefully. "I don't think people have to be the exact same to like each other. Do you?"

Ruby shrugged. "Well, it's a fact that people go a lot on looks. They figure that people who look like them are going to be the same, and people who look different are going to be different. From there it's pretty easy to jump to the conclusion that their difference isn't as good as your difference."

"Would you think that?" Kate asked, remembering perfectly well how Ruby had made up her mind right off that they were "white trash" just because they came that first day dressed in old clothes and not washed up or anything.

Ruby pushed Kate's left hand aside and reached for the right one. For a while she worked on the nails without saying anything. Just when Kate had given up on getting an answer, Ruby said, "When I first moved to New York, there was this Jewish girl who lived in the next apartment. I thought she was real strange. Like, she never went out on Friday nights. Her parents always came over. One hot Friday night I walked past and her apartment door was open. They were having supper together and doing this kind of ritual with candles and prayers and stuff. After that, when I passed her in the hall, it seemed like she was looking at me funny out of the corners of her eyes. I felt like telling her, 'Honey, you may think I'm weird, but I think you're pretty weird, too!'

"About a month later, we happened to ride up on the same elevator. She was looking at me out of the corners of her eyes again, and I was just about to blurt out something rude when she said, 'You know, you've got the most beautiful hair. I'd just love to learn how to do mine like that.'"

Ruby finished filing the nails on Kate's right hand and started buffing them. "I don't know that I thought I was better than her. But I did figure that because she never went out on Friday nights, and because the prayers at her supper table weren't like the ones Papa says at ours, we couldn't possibly have anything in common. But when I got to know her, turned out we read the same books and liked the same music and always wanted to see the same movies. We even had the same problems with our parents, who hadn't wanted us to move out on our own. So yeah, maybe I was a little prejudiced at first. At least, I prejudged her, which is more or less the same thing."

Kate frowned. "There's Jewish kids in our school. And kids from Latin America and the Caribbean, and way more Yankees than there used to be."

Ruby must have seen the frown, because she narrowed her eyes and asked, "Does that bother you?"

"Doesn't bother me that they're there," Kate said, flinching a little as Ruby dug under a fingernail again to get out a piece of dirt she'd missed. "It's how everybody gangs up against everybody else."

"You mean whites against blacks?" Ruby asked.

"Not only that," Kate told her. "The Latino kids from Puerto Rico fight with the Latinos from Cuba, and the American black kids make fun of black kids from Haiti, and white kids whose parents have regular jobs say terrible things about white kids on welfare. One day all the Baptist girls, black and white ones both, beat up a black girl who just moved here from Harlem when she said she was a Muslim and didn't believe in Jesus."

Ruby sighed. "That's exactly how I remember junior high. All cliques and us-against-them, even in this small town. And my parents couldn't understand why I hated school."

"I hate school, too," said Kate. Then she added, "But I like that story about you and your friend in New York. I think it's fun getting to know different kinds of people."

What Kate wanted to say, but didn't, was that the trouble wasn't her liking other people, it was getting other people to like *her*.

\*\*\*

At school the next day, when Kate looked at her manicured nails so smooth and clean and round, they made her feel good. The good feeling lasted all day long, right up till she climbed on the bus to go home. As she put her foot up on the first high step, she heard the sound of her too-tight jeans ripping. She reached back and felt the hole, and through it, her underpants.

She managed to get on the bus and into a seat without anybody noticing, and whispered to Chip to walk close behind her when she got off. As far as she could tell, nobody saw her underwear through the torn place. At least no one teased her about it.

Kate looked at the jeans when she got home to see if she could patch them, but the fabric was so worn she didn't think it would hold a patch. Not that she wanted a patch in the dead center of one cheek of a pair of too-tight jeans! Maybe Mom could think of something. Or else—Kate didn't know what. She could barely get her other jeans zipped anymore.

But Mom didn't come home at supper time. Instead, she called.

"Go ahead and eat without me," she told them. "We've got a cow down. Looks like a breech birth—you know, the calf's bottom is coming out first instead of its head. George has gone to town to see if he can find a vet. I've got to stay with the cow. It might be late when I get home."

Kate fell asleep with her book in her hand around midnight. It must have been really late when Mom got in. When Kate woke up the next morning, Mom was gone again, as usual, to do the morning milking. Kate rummaged through her clothes again, but couldn't find one thing to wear to school. Not church dresses; nobody ever wore dresses to school. Neither of her skirts would do either, nor any of the jeans. Two had broken zippers and two she couldn't zip at all.

Justin looked into Kate's room and saw her sitting there in her underwear, the torn jeans in her lap. "Hey! You're going to miss the bus."

"Leave me alone," Kate said, fighting to hold back tears.

Chip peeked in at her. "Come on, Kate," he said.

Justin gave Chip a push. "You come on, brat. No need for you to miss the bus just because Kate wants to."

Kate watched them walking up the driveway to Lost Goat Lane, and at the same time saw Luther and Ruby walking up the lane toward the bus stop out on the highway. Chip and

Luther ran to meet each other. Ruby said something to Justin. He pointed to the house.

The bus stopped and the boys got on. Ruby started back down the lane, walking slowly. Then, instead of continuing toward her own house, she turned down the Martin driveway, picking her way carefully around mud puddles left from rain in the night. She didn't come up on the porch, but walked over to the side of the house and spoke to Kate through the window.

"Hey girl. You missed the bus."

"I know."

"You sick?"

"No."

"What's wrong then?"

"My pants tore," Kate said.

"Guess you better pick out something else then," Ruby said. She started to walk away.

"Like what?" Kate almost screamed, then started to cry.

Ruby stopped. For a minute she stood there, looking down the driveway. Probably laughing at me, Kate thought miserably. Probably thinking how white trashy we are because I don't have twenty outfits like she probably has.

Ruby turned around. She wasn't laughing. "You must have *something*. Or we can fix the rip. Want me to take a look?"

"If you want," Kate mumbled.

Ruby came up on the porch. Kate stayed where she was, on the bed. She didn't particularly want Ruby seeing her with nothing on but a T-shirt and underwear. But Ruby walked right in through the front door and came down the hall to Kate's room. She stood in the doorway for a minute, looking around with a critical expression on her face. Anybody could tell from all the open dresser drawers and the way clothes were strewn about that Kate had been trying to find something to wear.

"How about shorts?"

"I don't have the right kind."

"What do you mean, 'the right kind'?" Ruby asked.

"They can't be cutoffs, and they've got to be down to your fingertips when you've got your arms straight down. All mine are shorter than that."

Ruby gave a short, un-funny laugh. "What about this?" she asked, picking up a skirt.

"I can barely get it buttoned. When I do it's so tight it hurts my stomach. But if I don't do the button it wrecks the zippers. Like those jeans." Kate jerked her head toward two pairs of jeans lying on the floor. Ruby picked them up and saw the broken zippers.

Ruby picked up a shirt missing two buttons and stared at it. "Does this ever take me back."

Kate glanced up at her. She had no idea what Ruby was talking about.

Ruby gave Kate a crooked smile. "I'll never forget the year I started popping buttons off everything. Booker teased me about being fat. The boys at school were always making jokes about my body. I'd sooner have gone to jail than to school that year. That's one of the reasons why I ran away from home."

Kate's mouth dropped open. How could anybody have teased somebody as gorgeous as Ruby about the way she looked? And teased her so badly that she had actually run away from home instead of going to school!

Ruby tossed the shirts aside and took the torn jeans from Kate. "Looks like these are beyond repair," she said, holding them up.

"That was my last pair," Kate said sadly. "The only ones that still fit right."

"Yeah, well." Ruby stuck her hand through the hole in Kate's pants and wiggled her fingers. She seemed to be thinking about something and couldn't quite make up her mind. Finally she said, "Why don't you come up to the house. Maybe I got a pair or two that would fit you."

"You mean—?" Kate didn't know what to say.

"I mean get your shorts on and let's go," Ruby said, flicking her long braids. "You don't want your mom to catch you ditching, do you?"

Kate grabbed a pair of cutoffs and was about to slip them on when she caught sight of herself next to Ruby in the mirror. Seeing her own skinny body next to Ruby's slender woman-curves made Kate feel hopeless. "But nothing's going to fit, Ruby. You're so... I'm so..."

"So what? You think it was breathing that ripped those pants? You're just growing, girl." Ruby slapped Kate lightly on the hip. "And in all the right places."

Ruby didn't say much on the walk to the Wilson house. A couple of times Kate glanced at her and wondered if Ruby was sorry she had gotten involved in what really wasn't her problem—maybe thinking about how she didn't want to give away any of her clothes after all. But when they got there Ruby cheered up. Kate cheered up, too. She was thankful that Mr. and Mrs. Wilson weren't around so she didn't have to explain to them why she wasn't in school.

"Come on back here," Ruby said, and headed down the hall.

"This your bedroom?" Kate asked shyly.

"Has been, ever since I was born," Ruby said. "Only thing that's changed is the bed. When I came back with Luther, we took out the double bed and put in twins. When Booker's not home, which is most of the time, Luther sleeps in his room. But when Booker comes for holidays, Luther sleeps there." She motioned toward one of the twin beds.

While she talked, Ruby rummaged through drawers stuffed with clothes. "Here, try these," she said, tossing Kate two pairs of jeans. "Up in New York, where I didn't have my mama's cooking to pig out on, I used to be a lot thinner than I am now, and I favored tight jeans. But I can't fit into these anymore. Somebody might as well get some use out of them."

Kate tried on both pairs of jeans, which were identical faded denim and just slightly flared at the bottom. They looked almost like her favorite jeans, the pair that had ripped.

Ruby leaned against the wall and looked at Kate critically. "A little long, but otherwise they fit okay."

"They look good on me," Kate said shyly.

"Yeah, well, looks are only half of it, and the little half at that. What really matters is how they feel. Because, honey, if you don't feel good, you're not going to look good, no matter what you're wearing."

That made sense to Kate; that's why she'd liked the torn jeans so much. They felt the same shape as her body.

Ruby rummaged in another drawer and tossed Kate a plain white shirt, just like the one Schroder had pinned the note on the back of, except that it was a size bigger. "Now, I just popped a button on this one," Ruby said. "But you haven't filled out all that much yet. Here, try it."

Kate buttoned it up and looked at herself in the mirror again.

"It'll do," Ruby decided. "But let me tell you something, Kate. When you look at yourself in the mirror, you want to see a girl looking back at you who's got her head held high. Her hair's shining clean—doesn't matter how it's fixed as long as it's clean, brushed till it really shines. And you're in what— seventh grade?"

Kate nodded.

"So there are girls in your class who smoke, right?" Before Kate could answer, Ruby said, "Just stay away from them when they're puffing."

"Why?" Kate actually thought the girls who smoked were kind of cool.

"Because they stink," Ruby said. "Their hair, their clothes, everything. If you spend five minutes in the bathroom with somebody who's smoking, you'll stink same as they do. I'm not saying be rude to them. Just don't hang around in air they've polluted."

"Okay," Kate promised. She figured she had enough problems without smelling bad, too.

"And don't go around slumping down like your breasts are something to hide." She gave Kate a jab between the shoulder blades that made Kate straighten up and stick out her chest. "There. See? You look okay. Not perfect—nobody's that—but okay. When somebody starts in on you, you just give them a look like, 'What are you, crazy? It's me that decides how good I look. And I say I look okay.'"

Kate took the jeans Ruby gave her home, then walked to school. She went straight to her homeroom teacher, Mrs. Bell, and explained how she'd missed the bus because her pants tore. Kate didn't lie, but she did tell it so it sounded like it happened at the last minute. Mrs. Bell wasn't the world's best teacher, because she was terrible at keeping order, but she was helpful if you had problems. Kate asked if she could do makeup work so as to not get marked absent for the two classes she'd missed, which would get her in trouble at home. Mrs. Bell said she'd speak to the other teachers, and Kate knew it was as good as done.

***

That very day Kate started using "the look," and it helped. Later, when she had time to practice it in front of her mirror, she got better at it. She still got hassled some, especially about her shoes, but on the whole there wasn't as much teasing as before.

But mostly what made it easier was that even though she still didn't have any friends at school, at least she had Ruby. Kate could never figure out whether Ruby took the time to talk to her only because she was bored or if she was really starting to like her. All Kate knew was that Ruby was nicer than she used to be.

Kate never told Mom about the jeans. Mom wasn't at home when Kate and her brothers left for school in the morning, and by the time the bus dropped them off in the afternoon, she was getting ready for work and usually in a rush. Kate either hung around outside until she was gone, or if Mom was outside, Kate waved and went straight to her room and took off the jeans Ruby had given her.

Only once did Mom seem to notice anything different. She frowned and said, "Katie, have you lost weight?"

Even though the jeans Ruby had given her were the same shape and faded blue as her own, they weren't as tight. "No ma'am," she said, and scooted into her bedroom.

Kate wasn't sure why she didn't want Mom to know that Ruby had given her clothes. Partly it was because she didn't want Mom to get upset all over again about not having the money to buy them new school clothes this year. And partly it was because she didn't know how to explain Ruby to Mom. How could she tell her that Ruby wasn't a real friend, just almost a friend? And Kate was pretty sure that Mom wouldn't like her taking clothes from neighbors she didn't know all that well. So she just kept quiet about it.

# 6

# Hurricane

By the end of October Kate was having fewer problems at school, but it seemed like Justin was having more. Nobody understood exactly what was going on with him. The principal sent Mom a letter that called Justin "sullen" and "uncooperative." After Mom read the letter aloud, she asked Justin what was going on. He shrugged and sat there looking sullen and uncooperative till Mom gave up trying to talk to him.

One day Justin even got detention from Mr. Jackson.

"I thought you liked Mr. Jackson," Kate said to her brother the next morning. "You said he was the best math teacher you ever had."

"What difference does that make?" Justin asked, and walked away leaving Kate to wonder, like everybody else, what was bugging him.

Luckily Justin wasn't Kate's problem. She was only responsible for Chip, and looking after Chip was a lot easier now. Every afternoon he walked home with Luther as soon as they got off the bus, and they did their homework together. That gave Kate some quiet time after school to get her own homework done.

But Kate hadn't allowed Chip to go home with Luther this particular afternoon, and he was being a real pain. Every five minutes he whined, "I want to go over to Luther's."

"No, Chip!" Kate said for the fourth time. "It's raining too hard."

"Luther might be scared," Chip fretted. "He's never been in a hurricane."

Hoping for some support, Kate looked over at Justin. He was at Mom's desk supposedly doing his homework, but so far as Kate could tell he was just staring out the window. "It's not going to hit the mainland," he said. "All we're getting is rain and a little more wind than usual."

Kate looked out the window and then at the clock. Only four-thirty. "Look how dark it's getting. We better get the chores done."

"Yeah," Justin agreed. He got up from the desk and was just reaching for the radio to turn it off when a news announcer broke in, talking fast in an excited voice. "Hurricane Lila, which was headed out to sea, has changed course and is moving toward the mainland at a speed of ten to fifteen miles an hour. It is expected to hit the Florida coast in the vicinity of Palm Beach in approximately three hours, with winds in excess of eighty miles per hour."

"Did you hear that?" Chip looked really worried. "He said eighty miles an hour. That's really bad, isn't it?"

"It'll be fine, Chip," Kate said. "Come on and help us get everything ready."

They'd been through hurricanes before, but in the past Mom had always been there to take care of things. In fact, she had gotten the storm shutters out yesterday and put up the ones along the back of the house where the windows were highest. But when the radio said the hurricane was going to pass them by and Southern Florida would only get heavy rain, she'd decided not to bother with the rest. Kate didn't think there was a radio in the dairy barn, which meant Mom probably didn't know the hurricane had changed course and was headed toward them. But it was a big, well-built barn. As long as she was there, she'd be okay. But in the meantime, they were on their own. They'd have to get everything done before the hurricane hit.

They hurried out to the back porch and put on their yellow rain ponchos. When Justin opened the door, the wind blew it back so hard it nearly knocked him down. They ducked their heads and ran down the steps into a dark gray world of wind and stinging rain.

Normally it only took two people to put up a storm shutter, one to climb the ladder and one on the ground to pass the shutter up so the person on the ladder could fasten it in place. Kate passed the first shutter up to Justin, but he could barely hold on to it. Then a gust of wind blew the shutter, the ladder, and Justin down in a pile, with Justin on the bottom.

That's when Kate thought of using the big wooden crate. Fortunately all the windows in front were low, because their house didn't have an upstairs. By putting the crate under a window and standing on it, the three of them together could just barely hold the shutter in place long enough to get it fastened. Justin hooked it at the top while Kate and Chip held it, then Kate fastened the middle hooks and Chip did the bottom ones. They moved the crate from one window to the next until all the windows were covered with the strong wooden shutters Dad had built years ago.

They had just gotten the last window covered and stepped down from the crate when they heard a screech of metal. The wind tore a sheet of tin off the duck coop and smashed it against the storm shutter they had just put up. For a few seconds the tin was pinned against the side of the house by the wind. Then it fell to the ground, barely missing them.

Suddenly Kate realized how dangerous the hurricane really was. If they had been standing on the crate when the sharp sheet of metal came sailing through the air, it could have cut all three of them right in half.

Justin pointed to the roof and made a lifting motion. Kate understood. He meant that they'd gotten the shutter in place just in time. If the tin had smashed the window, it would have let the wind into the house. When a hurricane-force wind gets inside a house, it can rip the whole roof right off.

They were about to make a dash for the back door when Kate saw that one side of the duck coop had blown off. The big white ducks were huddled together against the back wall. Rain pounded them and the wind was blowing their feathers every which way. She motioned to Justin to pick up the other end of the crate. They carried it over to what was left of the duck coop and started putting ducks into the crate. The ducks quacked nervously, but when Chip patted them they squatted down in the crate and stayed there, where at least they had a little protection from the wind.

Justin and Kate lugged the crate full of ducks toward the house. As they passed Sugar's shed Kate realized that the storm might blow it down. She shouted to Chip, "Bring Sugar, too!"

"Get the back door open!" Justin yelled.

Chip grabbed Sugar by the collar and ran to open the back door, holding one hand over his eyes to keep out the stinging rain. Kate pushed Sugar ahead of them into the kitchen. She and Justin staggered in with the crate of ducks and set it down on the floor next to the stove.

Chip tried to close the door behind them, but the wind was too strong. When Kate and Justin went back to help, they saw the calves. The wind had forced them against the fence. The panicked animals were pushing against the wire so hard it was about to break. Any second the wire would snap and all three calves would be running wild on the highway.

"Got to bring them in!" Justin yelled.

They managed to pull the door shut, then plunged back out into the wind and rain. They got a rope around the neck of the first calf, but it wasn't used to being led. When Justin pulled on the rope, it braced its feet and wouldn't budge. Kate and Chip got behind and pushed. Little by little they worked it across the yard and up the back steps into the kitchen.

Kate lined up the dinette chairs to keep the calf barricaded on one side of the kitchen. Justin ran out to the goat shed and returned with an armful of hay. He threw the hay in the corner and helped Kate turn the table on its side to make a better pen. Then they ran back to the corral for another calf.

The drainage ditch on the far side of the corral was overflowing. The second calf ran wildly from one side of the soggy pasture to the other, with the children sloshing along behind it. When Kate and Chip tried to block its way so Justin could get the rope on it, the calf ran right into them. Chip got knocked down and trampled in the mud. At last Justin caught the calf and dragged it toward the house with Kate and Chip pushing from behind.

Actually Chip wasn't any help at all. He had a cut on his forehead and was crying. "They're stomping all over me," he wailed as Kate pushed the calf through the back door into the kitchen and pulled it shut again.

"Then stay here," Kate said. "Or get some more hay." She and Justin ran back to the corral to get the last calf.

The air was filled with banging and screeching noises as more sheets of tin ripped loose from the sheds and sailed past, their deadly sharp edges slashing through the air like monster knives. The last calf ran in terror from one end of the pen to another as if Justin wasn't the same boy who fed it every day, but some devil blown in by the storm. When Justin finally got a rope on the calf, it dashed in a crazed circle, tangling Justin's feet in the rope and knocking Kate backwards. Black water from the overflowing ditch closed over her head.

She came up sputtering. Justin got his feet untangled, stood up, and tugged on the rope as hard as he could. Kate got her hands on the calf's slippery wet behind and pushed. Fighting the calf was bad enough, but fighting the wind was even harder. They could barely stand up against it. When it blew full force, they couldn't move forward at all. But the wind came in gusts, and when it let up for a second or two, they were able to drag the calf forward a few feet.

They had almost reached the house when a branch from one of the trees in the front yard cracked overhead like a gunshot. The calf covered the rest of the distance to the house in a few huge leaps, dragging Justin with it. That's when Kate heard Chip scream. She saw him lying in a mud puddle, holding the armful of hay he had brought from the goat shed. Every time he tried to get up the wind blew him down. Kate fought her way through the wind to get to him.

"Leave the hay," she shouted as she helped Chip to his feet and hung onto him. Together they struggled back to the house.

Justin was just inside the back door, pulling hard to bring the calf in after him, while the calf was pulling just as hard in the opposite direction. Kate pushed the calf and Chip ahead of her until they tumbled onto the back porch in a muddy heap.

They were soaking wet and breathless, but they were out of the awful wind. They rested a moment, then got the last calf into the kitchen.

It was black dark by then and the electricity was off. Justin lit one of the fat, long-burning candles that Mom kept especially for hurricanes. If they had wanted to fix supper they could have because the stove and hot water heater were both gas, but they were too exhausted to be hungry. After they washed up and changed into dry clothes, Kate made some hot chocolate.

They drank the cocoa sitting in the middle of the kitchen floor. The calves were lying down in the corner, penned in by the turned-over table and chairs. The ducks were asleep in the crate with their heads tucked under their wings. Sugar was the only animal still awake. She lay quietly among them, watching everything with bright, curious eyes.

Kate noticed Chip shivering. "You better go to bed," she said.

Chip ignored her and crawled into the hay next to the calves. Kate realized that with Mom not home yet and with the wind howling so loud, Chip was probably scared to be alone in his room. Kate went and got their sleeping bags from the closet. She tossed one to Chip and one to Justin.

"I think we should stay here in the kitchen with the animals," she said, "to keep them calmed down."

Kate wrapped up in her own sleeping bag and lay down next to Sugar. The last thing she thought of, before falling into a doze, was that Mom might not be able to get home at all. The road might be flooded, or the wind might blow the car off the road, or a fallen tree might block…

When Kate heard banging on the back porch, for a minute she didn't know if it was something in a dream or something hitting the house, or what. Then the door opened and Mom was standing there. She had kicked off her boots on the back porch and stood barefoot. Water dripped off her hair, off her nose, off everything, and puddled around her.

Justin scrambled to his feet and helped Mom take off her raincoat. He looked at her soaking wet clothes and grinned. "Raincoat didn't do you much good, did it?"

Kate couldn't tell if the water streaming down Mom's face was rain or tears. It took her a minute to see that it was both. Mom was laughing and crying at the same time.

"You're safe!" Mom gasped. "And you've rescued every last animal!"

"We were worried about you," Kate said.

"I was in the milking barn," Mom explained. "It wasn't till I let the first batch of cows out that I noticed how much the wind had picked up. George turned on the radio in his pickup and got a weather report. As soon as he heard the hurricane had changed directions he sent me home. But by then there were trees down and flooded places I didn't dare cross for fear the car would stall. I had to keep backtracking and I ended up circling all the way around by the Buchanan place."

Kate sat up. "We were too tired to make supper, but I saved you some hot chocolate."

"Darling Kate!" Mom whispered. "You're wonderful!"

Mom knelt next to Chip, who was still asleep, and kissed the cut on his forehead.

Then she put her arm around Kate and looked up at Justin. "There's not one in a million who could do what you kids did tonight," she said. "I hope you will always remember that."

# 7
# Kate Alone

Chip didn't wake up even when Mom carried him to bed. Justin lit another candle and stuck it on the back of the toilet so Mom could see to take her bath. Then he went to bed.

Kate warmed up the hot chocolate. Carrying two cups, she went to the bathroom door. "Mom?" she called. "Want some hot chocolate?"

"You bet I do! Come on in, honey."

Mom was in the tub looking as if she'd like to stay there soaking in the hot bath forever. Her long blonde hair was down, trailing in the water. It was already so wet that it didn't matter if it got a little wetter. Kate sat down on the floor with her back against the tub, and together they sipped their cocoa.

Mom put her hand out and stroked Kate's hair, which was still damp. Kate glanced over her shoulder at Mom's face. Mom smiled at her in a way that made Kate think this was the most special moment they had ever had together.

There are times not to tell your parents what's on your mind, and times to tell them everything. Kate felt like this was the time to tell Mom all the things she'd been keeping secret.

"We brought Sugar in first," Kate said, "because she's going to have a baby."

Mom chuckled. "That goat of yours eats like a pig. She's not pregnant; she's just fat."

"No, Mom. She's going to have a baby."

Mom was still smiling. "What makes you think so?"

"Mr. Wilson said."

"Who?"

"Mr. Wilson. You know, he has that big white billy…"

The sentence died in Kate's throat because Mom had stopped smiling. Instead of looking pleased, she was looking upset.

Kate got her voice back and said quickly, "Billy's a real good goat. He takes first prize every year at the fair."

"Look, Katie, we cannot afford—"

"We already paid," Kate explained. "With duck eggs. Mrs. Wilson says they're better than regular for baking. And Ruby says—"

"Ruby?" Mom interrupted.

"The Wilsons' daughter."

"The one who dropped out of school and ran away from home?" Mom stood up and reached for a towel, which she wrapped around herself.

"Ruby," Kate repeated. "Who used to live in New York but now she's come home, her and Luther, and—"

"Is this the same Luther that Chip talks about all the time?"

"Well, yes."

"I thought Luther was somebody in Chip's class."

"He is. He's the Wilsons' grandson and he's in Chip's class. He's Chip's best friend."

"How do you know these people?" Mom asked. There was a sharpness in her voice that made Kate nervous and caused her to stumble, not sure exactly how to explain something that a second ago had seemed so simple.

"Well, uh, we just go there and—"

"Go there?" Mom demanded. "When do you go there?"

"Uh, well, Chip usually walks home with Luther after school, but Justin and I have our own homework to do, so we mostly go on weekends."

"What about Chip's homework?"

"I told you," Kate said impatiently. "Chip and Luther are in the same grade. They have Ruby and Mr. and Mrs. Wilson all three to help them. When I have to help Chip, it takes so long sometimes I don't even get my own homework done!"

"Kate," Mom said in a voice so sharp Kate felt as if she'd been slapped. "It is your responsibility to look after Chip, yours and Justin's. I do not want you kids going down there every day. I don't want the neighbors to think I can't look after my own children."

"I just thought…" Kate started in a small voice. Then all the excitement and fear and exhaustion of the night flooded in on her. She felt as if it was impossible to explain anything. "Never mind," she said. She got up and went out of the bathroom with a tight ache in her chest. It was the most special moment she and Mom had ever had, and it had barely lasted one minute. Mom didn't even seem to care that Sugar was going to have a baby.

Kate climbed into bed and lay there listening to the wind howling and the rain pounding against the house. With the electricity off and no moon or stars and wooden shutters covering the windows, it was the blackest darkness Kate could remember.

She saw a wavering light in the hall and knew it was Mom, carrying the candle. She stopped at Kate's door and whispered, "Katie?"

Kate pretended to be asleep, and in a second Mom went on down the hall to her own room.

# Kate Alone

Kate didn't know why she had pretended to be asleep. But she had thought it was a good time to talk to Mom, and it turned out not to be. Maybe there would never be a good time.

When the light disappeared, Kate knew Mom had blown out the candle and gone to bed. Kate got up and tiptoed into the kitchen. She heard a couple of little *click-click-click* steps. Sugar was no longer lying down. Kate felt around in the dark until she found a sleeping bag. Then she took hold of Sugar's collar and led her back to her bedroom.

Kate knew that in the morning she'd find little round marbles of poop on the floor, but she didn't care. She spread the sleeping bag next to her bed and climbed into it, then tapped the back of Sugar's knees. The goat folded her thin legs and lay down next to Kate on the floor.

Kate put her hand against Sugar's soft belly and waited. In a moment she felt a small kick from inside, and then another, and another. Kate smiled. This baby was all legs. Either that or it was twins.

# 8
# Chip Alone

By morning the hurricane wind had passed, but it was still raining. There was no school because so many of the streets were flooded or blocked by blown-down trees and other debris. It was just as well Kate and her brothers stayed home, because there was a lot of work to do. The animals were still penned up in the kitchen, which was beginning to smell pretty bad. Mom had left early like she always did, and she didn't come home from the dairy at noon because they had to clean up some hurricane damage there, too.

In the afternoon, when the rain finally stopped, Kate threw down fresh hay in Sugar's shed and put her back in her pen. Then she and Justin set about getting the calves back to their corral. By then the calves were used to the warm, dry kitchen and didn't want to leave. Justin had to drag each one down the back steps with Kate pushing from behind. But once a calf got down the steps, it ran for the pasture so fast that Kate and Justin could barely keep up.

Next Kate and Justin gathered up the sheets of tin that had blown off the duck coop. Chip disappeared. Kate figured he had gone down to see Luther. He hadn't said he was going, so she didn't have to mention what Mom had said about their visiting the Wilsons. Anyway, she was glad not to have to look after him for a couple of hours. It was hard work dragging the big sheets of tin from wherever they had blown, and even harder to hold them into place while Justin nailed them back on the duck coop where they belonged.

After a while Chip came back, and Luther was with him. "Guess what?" Chip said, breathless. "We saw a cottonmouth water moccasin!"

"It was shiny black!" exclaimed Luther. "It opened its mouth and flicked its little black tongue at us, and we saw the inside, all white."

"I hope you know how poisonous cottonmouths are," Justin said. "With water all over the place there's no telling where they might be, so you be careful where you step!"

"You think we're stupid?" Chip shot back. Chip hated being told things he already knew.

Justin ignored Chip and started banging nails into the tin. "Don't know why we're bothering to fix this junky shed," he muttered. "It's not like we're going to be here that much longer."

Kate looked around quickly to see if Luther had heard. She didn't want the Wilsons to know that the bank might take the farm because they were behind on the payments. Although it wasn't her fault, she felt ashamed. She was relieved to see Chip and Luther halfway up the lane, headed off on some private mission of their own.

"Justin," she said, "is that why you aren't keeping up your grades? Because you think we might have to change schools if—?"

He gave the nail a vicious whack. "That's right. Even if I got straight A's I couldn't go out for the baseball team, because we're not going to be here."

"We might not have to change schools," Kate argued. "There's only the one high school in our district. Wherever we move, it'll probably be someplace close by."

"Kate! If we lose the farm," he yelled, banging the hammer hard every few words, "there's no way Mom's going to stick around here and let people feel sorry for us. She'd hate that." *Bam!* "She'll want to move to where nobody knows us." *Bam!* "And even if she didn't, I would." *Bam! Bam! Bam!*

Kate didn't answer. In the first place, Justin was hammering so hard on the tin that he couldn't have heard her, and in the second place, she didn't know what to say anyway. Mom had assured her that they weren't going to lose the farm. Justin seemed sure they would. The way it looked to Kate, neither one of them really knew what was going to happen.

When there were enough nails in the tin that Kate didn't need to hold it in place anymore, she walked away. She had that same terrible feeling she used to get when Justin talked about leaving, only worse. Much worse, because now she was thinking that maybe *all* of them would be leaving.

She went back into the house and cleaned up the kitchen, which was a mess after a goat, three calves, and a dozen ducks had slept there. Even after it was clean it smelled like a barn, but with the window open and fresh air blowing through, Kate figured it would be nearly normal by supper time.

After that Kate went to milk Sugar. She saw Justin out feeding the calves, but Chip hadn't come back yet. She picked her way across the debris-strewn yard, annoyed that Chip had run off to play with Luther when there was so much to do. He could have helped pick up some of the broken limbs and stuff, and he definitely should have come home in time to get the ducks fed and the eggs gathered, since those were his chores. If he wasn't back by the time she finished the milking she'd have to walk down to the Wilsons' to get him, which meant Justin would have to fix supper by himself, when that was supposed to be everybody's job.

Kate was just coming out of the goat shed with a pail of foaming warm milk when she saw Chip and Luther out on Lost Goat Lane, coming from the direction of the highway. They separated, Luther heading for his house and Chip coming up the driveway toward her.

It occurred to Kate that Chip disappeared quite often nowadays. Used to be he never went anywhere by himself, only tagged along with her and Justin. But now that he and Luther had become friends—no, even before that—ever since the alligator got Go-Boy, Chip had taken to going off on his own.

For a minute Kate wondered whether Chip might've gotten up his nerve to go back to the big canal. She sure hoped he hadn't gone off toward the big canal again. A gator that big, if it got a chance, could catch a child as easy as a dog.

# 9
# Justin Alone

A few days after the hurricane, Mom had a "family conference." She started by telling Justin, Kate, and Chip how important it was that they had managed to save the animals. It was especially important because they were still having serious money problems.

"I don't see how we can have money problems when you're working seven days a week," Justin said sourly.

Mom made them all get a pencil and paper and do arithmetic—a budget, she called it—to see what happened to the money she earned.

"I make minimum wage," she explained. "After taxes, I bring home about $1000 a month." They all wrote $1000 on their papers. "Now subtract $600, which is the mortgage payment I have to make to the bank."

That was easy. Even Chip could figure out that after the mortgage payment, they'd have $400 left.

"Out of that I have to pay the utilities, buy feed for the animals and food for ourselves, and pay for gas and car insurance. I also have to keep up the health insurance payments in case anybody gets sick."

Mom told them how much each thing cost per month. They

subtracted the amounts she called out until they were right down to zero.

"Can't you work out something with the bank?" Justin asked. "Maybe smaller payments or something?"

"I tried," Mom said, her voice getting tight and angry. "Your father and I took out this mortgage fifteen years ago, and it's real close to being paid off. So I asked the bank to give me a one-year extension. One year, that was all I asked. But there's a new manager at the bank who doesn't know me from Adam and doesn't care. He's not a people person like the old manager. This one, all he does is look at the numbers on the application and tell me my income's too small and I don't qualify. Not even for an extension. So I'm telling you now, we're going to be living hand-to-mouth until I get caught up on the payments. We simply cannot lose this farm."

"Or the animals," Chip put in.

"Or the animals," Mom repeated. Her lower lip was pushed out and her face was dead serious.

Kate looked at Mom's determined face and felt just as determined. She didn't know how she could help them keep the farm, but if there was any way, she'd do it.

Justin said nothing. He just stared at the numbers as if it was hopeless. If somebody told Justin he couldn't do something, he just gave up.

He hadn't always been like that. When he was little he acted like he could do anything, and Kate, two years younger, really believed he could. But after Mom gave them the news that Dad was never coming back, the confidence seemed to drain right out of Justin.

"I think I can catch up the payments," Mom said, continuing to write down numbers. "But there's going to be very little money for other things. That's why we want to raise as much of our own food as much as we can." She smiled around the table at all of them. "Sugar and the ducks give us food. Next spring we can sell the calves and use that money to buy things we need. In the meantime..." Mom gave Kate and Justin a hard look. "...I'm counting on you to stay home and take good care of each other and your little brother."

"Yes ma'am," Kate said, looking down at the numbers on the page, which started out with $1000 and ended up with a big fat zero.

Kate never got around to telling Chip and Justin that Mom had said they shouldn't visit the Wilsons anymore. And actually Mom hadn't said they shouldn't *ever* go there. All she'd said was, "I don't want you going down there every day."

Well, Kate didn't go there every day. She never had. And Chip didn't know he wasn't supposed to, so he kept on walking home with Luther after school. On weekends they all went to the Wilsons, sometimes in the morning, before Mom got home from the dairy, and sometimes in the afternoon, after she'd gone back for the evening milking. They never stayed long. And Kate made sure that they always got home before Mom did, so there wouldn't be any questions about where they'd been.

Kate had learned long ago that once Chip knew something was a secret, he had a hard time keeping it. In fact, if he got mad, he might tell on purpose. The best thing was to not say anything and hope he wouldn't either.

For a while that had worked well. Although Chip often said "Luther this" or "Luther that," he went a whole month without saying anything about the rest of the Wilson family.

The day before Booker was supposed to come, just before Thanksgiving, Chip was so excited about Booker coming that as he climbed up on his step stool to dry the dishes, he started babbling. "Luther says Booker can hit a ball one mile and he can—"

"Oh, Chip," Justin said, rinsing a handful of soapy silverware and tossing it in the dish drainer. "Nobody can hit a ball one mile."

"You'll see," Chip argued. "You'll see when we go over there tomorrow—"

Kate was sweeping the floor. She had just opened her mouth to say, "Hush, Chip!" when Mom walked through the kitchen.

"There's no need for you kids to go over there tomorrow," Mom said.

Justin stopped washing dishes. Chip stopped drying. Kate stopped sweeping.

"But Mom, we have to," Chip explained. "Booker's coming tomorrow."

"He's coming to spend time with his family, and they won't be wanting you kids hanging around." Mom headed for the living room. Over her shoulder she said, "We'll have our own Thanksgiving dinner day after tomorrow, a nice roast chicken. And Kate, I got the ingredients for pumpkin pie. That'll keep you plenty busy. So don't be looking for excuses to go over to the Wilsons' this weekend, you hear me?"

Justin looked as if he had been hit in the face. He threw the dishcloth in the sink and walked out the back door.

"Hey!" Chip yelled. "You're not finished." Then his eyes filled with tears.

"Shhhh," Kate whispered. "Don't worry. We'll find a way."

She put her hands in the warm soapy water and started washing dishes, not so much to help out as to have a few minutes to think what to do.

They could just wait till Mom had gone to work, then go to

the Wilsons' like they always did. But it was not a good idea to do something Mom had told them not to do. They'd learned that much when they hung out at the big canal after she had forbidden it. It would be better to explain the situation with the Wilsons and get permission. But when Mom had told them to stay home this weekend she'd sounded like she wasn't in a mood to discuss it.

Kate was all the way through the pots and pans when it suddenly hit her that if Mom didn't change her mind, something really bad might happen. The real problem was Justin. He was still having trouble at school. He hardly ever spoke to anybody, and he told Kate he didn't need friends. Half the time he didn't bother to do his homework. He usually just sat around in the afternoon reading books about far-off places. Kate knew what was on his mind. Not getting to meet Booker would be the last straw. Justin might really run away from home.

The minute the thought came into Kate's mind, she dashed out the back door. For a moment she didn't see Justin in the darkness and thought maybe he had already run away. Then she saw him in the front yard. He was standing with his hands hanging limp at his sides, watching cars go by on the highway. He didn't even have a baseball in his hand.

Kate went and stood beside him. He didn't seem to notice her.

"Please don't run away," Kate said.

"Why run away?" he asked in a dull voice. "We're going to get kicked out of here in a few months anyway."

"You don't know that!" Kate cried. "Mom said—"

"I know what she said," he interrupted. "But why do you think she doesn't want us to get friendly with the Wilsons? Because she knows we'll be moving, that's why. She doesn't want to have to tell neighbors that our property's getting repossessed."

Justin walked away into the darkness. When car headlights flashed by she saw him watching the calves lying down in a corner of their pen. Kate talked to Sugar while she milked her, telling her what a mess things were. She knew Chip talked to the ducks, using a soft, quacky voice that was almost like theirs. But Justin didn't talk to animals. He didn't talk to anybody. Justin was just...alone.

Kate went back into the house. She found Mom at the desk, her head bent over the bills. There couldn't be a worse time to bother her, but Kate knew she had to. She stood awhile before her mom looked up.

"What is it, Katie?"

"Mom, are we going to lose the farm?"

"No." Mom went back to writing checks. After a minute she looked up again and said in an impatient voice, "What is it, Katie?"

"Booker Wilson's the best ballplayer who ever lived in this town."

"I know that," Mom said, continuing to write checks. Finally she looked up again. "So?"

"Justin's really scared." Kate couldn't tell Mom that he, and in fact all of them, were still scared of losing the farm—not after she told them it wouldn't happen. "About...about not making the baseball team next spring."

"He's certainly not going to make the team if he doesn't get his grades up," her mom said unsympathetically.

"Getting to meet Booker Wilson would be, well, it would make Justin feel better. Maybe seeing somebody from our high school who actually played pro ball would inspire him to try harder."

Mom didn't answer right away, but she did stop writing. She stared off into space with a little smile on her face, as if she was thinking about something that made her feel good.

"Did you ever get to see him play ball?" Kate asked.

Mom blinked and looked at Kate like she was just remembering she was there. "Yes," she said. "I've seen Booker play ball."

"So can we go meet him? Mr. Wilson invited us."

"He invited you? You're sure?"

"Yes ma'am."

"All right," Mom said. Her voice turned sharp. "But just long enough to say hello, you hear me? Then you kids come straight home."

"Thanks, Mom!"

Kate dashed out of the room before her mom could change her mind again. As she raced through the kitchen, she gave Chip a thumbs-up sign to let him know it was okay. Then she went outside to look for Justin. He was standing right where he had been before, over by the calf pen, all by himself.

"Justin!" she called softly. "It's okay! We can go!"

Justin turned around. "Really?"

"Yeah. Really."

He lifted his arms and with a huge smile, swung an imaginary bat at an imaginary ball.

Kate knew what that meant: *Home run!*

# 10

# Booker and Everybody

Kate didn't even think about going home when they got off the bus on Wednesday afternoon, but hurried along with Luther, Chip, and Justin to the Wilsons' house. The quicker they got there the better chance they'd have of being there when Booker arrived—and the less chance that Mom would change her mind. When they arrived, Luther flung his book bag on the front porch and climbed onto the top of a tire swing. Chip gave the swing a push. Justin headed around the side of the house to Mr. Wilson's shop, and Kate stepped up onto the porch to go inside.

"Uncle Booker's here!" Luther yelled. Chip grabbed the tire and Luther jumped off. Kate and Justin hurried to the front yard.

A blue van sped along Lost Goat Lane. As it got closer, Kate could make out the driver, a man with big shoulders and the widest grin she had ever seen.

By the time the van came to a complete stop, Luther, Ruby, and Mrs. Wilson were clustered at the driver's door, each trying to be the first to hug Booker. Mr. Wilson unloaded Booker's bags. Kate stood on the far side of the van with Justin and Chip, waiting to be introduced. When Booker finally got free of his family's hugs and came around the van to where they were standing, Kate couldn't believe what she saw.

This was Booker Wilson, the most famous baseball player who ever lived in this town? *The* Booker Wilson who was now a coach in Atlanta? That was impossible! Booker Wilson was in a wheelchair!

At least Kate kept her wits about her and remembered not to stare. Justin was so surprised his mouth fell open.

Booker glared at him. "What you staring at, boy?"

"You don't—" Justin started to say, then remembered himself, and snapped his mouth shut.

*"What?"* Booker yelled. "What are you meaning to say? I don't have any *feet?"*

Booker not only didn't have feet, he didn't have much in the way of legs either. What legs he did have ended at the knees, which stuck straight out in front of him. He wore blue jeans, like anybody might, but they were cut off short, like his legs, and sewed up at the bottom.

Booker slipped his hand into the side pocket of his wheelchair and with a lightning movement, threw a baseball hard and fast, right at Justin. Justin was quick and got his hand up in time to catch the ball. But Kate could tell by the way Justin kept rubbing his hand on his pants afterward that it stung like crazy.

"Guess you got a notion that a person with no feet can't be involved in sports," Booker said, still glaring at Justin. "Well, let me tell you something." He looked from Justin to Kate to Chip. "It's way smarter to mind what people *do* have than what they don't!"

Booker spun his wheelchair around and headed toward the back of the van. "Hey, Luther," he yelled. "I got a bicycle in here, if somebody will help me lift it out."

# Booker and Everybody

Mr. Wilson opened the back door of the van and said, "Give us a hand here, Justin."

Justin reached in and lifted the bike out—if you could call it a bike. It looked like a piece of junk to Kate.

"It's got no pedals!" Luther exclaimed.

"No chain either," said Chip.

"You going to fix it?" Kate asked doubtfully. "Frame's pretty bent."

Booker stared at the bicycle as if he had never noticed its problems. He looked hurt.

Justin looked at Booker's down-turned mouth, then back at the bike. "Looks like it was in an accident," Justin said. "The wheels are good, though. Practically new."

Booker rocked back in his wheelchair and grinned at Justin. "By golly, but you are a quick study, my man! No point in whining about what we don't have. We're going to do something with what we got. How about carrying this thing around to Papa's shop?"

Justin didn't smile, but Kate could tell that he was pleased with Booker's response. Her brother hefted the bicycle to his shoulder and carried it out to the shed Mr. Wilson used for a workshop.

Booker followed in his wheelchair with Luther running along on one side, Chip on the other. Mr. and Mrs. Wilson and Ruby walked just behind them and Kate brought up the rear. Already Kate could tell there was something about Booker that made you want to stick close to him. He acted like something really interesting might happen any minute.

The crate-like thing was still on Mr. Wilson's workbench. Kate had never paid much attention to it. She now saw that it had an axle and two shafts: everything needed to make it a cart except wheels.

87

Booker asked, "Did you find a harness, Papa?"

Mr. Wilson lifted a leather harness off a hook on the wall and held it up. "Think this'll do?"

"Beautiful!" Booker grinned. "Luther, you and your friend bring old Billy over here and let's see how he likes it."

He turned to Justin. "Want to give me a hand getting these wheels off?"

Mr. Wilson handed Booker and Justin each a wrench.

"Heaven's sake, Sam!" Mrs. Wilson said to her husband. "Our boy's not got the road dust off and you've set him to work!"

"I was only—" Mr. Wilson tried to protest, but Mrs. Wilson didn't give him a chance to finish. She patted Booker's broad shoulder.

"Aren't you hungry, son?"

"You better be." Ruby put her hands on her hips. "Because we've been cooking for two days!"

"Hungry?" Booker rolled his eyes. "Ladies, I'm so hungry I could eat old Billy without barbecue sauce. It'll just take us a minute to see if this contraption works, then I'll be right in."

Mrs. Wilson laughed. "Come on, Ruby," she said, heading for the house. "That's one desperately hungry man. Let's get dinner on the table."

Booker started taking one wheel off the bicycle. Justin watched him a minute, then went to work removing the other one. When they had both wheels off, Mr. Wilson fitted them onto the cart. Then he and Justin lifted the cart off the workbench and turned it right-side-up. Chip and Luther returned leading Billy. When they saw the waiting cart, they started laughing. They were finally figuring out what Kate had figured out fifteen minutes ago: the bicycle wasn't meant to be a bicycle for Luther, but part of a goat cart. Even Billy must have sensed what was going on, because he started tossing his head and prancing like he was on parade. Kate held him while Mr. Wilson buckled him into the new harness. The boys pulled the cart up behind Billy and Mr. Wilson attached the harness to the shaft.

"Kate," said Mr. Wilson. "Go over there by the water faucet where I was washing vegetables from the garden and bring me some carrot tops. We might have to bribe Billy to behave himself till he gets used to his new responsibilities."

Kate ran to do as she was told. As she passed under the kitchen window she heard Ruby say, "Woman at the door. Some white woman."

Kate knew who the white woman was before she got to the side of the porch and the water faucet, because she could see her mom's car parked out front. Kate knew she should have left for work by now, but she must have waited just to be sure they came straight home like they promised after saying hello to Booker. Which of course they hadn't. Now she was standing at the screen door with a brown paper bag.

"Why hello, Mrs. Martin." Mrs. Wilson pushed open the screen door. "Won't you come in?"

"No, thank you," Mom said. "I just came to get my children and—"

Mrs. Wilson called over her shoulder, "Come out here, Ruby. It's the children's mama." Mrs. Wilson came out onto the porch, Ruby behind her. "Mrs. Martin, you remember our daughter Ruby?"

"Don't believe I would have recognized you," Mom said to Ruby. "Must be ten years since I saw you last."

Ruby barely nodded at Mom, without smiling or saying hi or anything like that.

"The children are around back," Mrs. Wilson explained.

"Booker's helping them rig up a goat cart."

"Kate said he was coming home for Thanksgiving. I didn't want them to intrude on your family get-together, but Justin just had to meet Booker. I told them they could visit for a minute, but you know kids. They can't tell a minute from an hour." Mom hesitated, then shoved the paper bag into Mrs. Wilson's hands. "And I wanted to give you this."

"What's this?" Mrs. Wilson sounded uncertain about taking whatever Mom was handing her.

"I get all the butter I want from the dairy," Mom explained. "It being the holidays and all, I thought you could use some extra."

"Like the duck eggs, I guess," Ruby said, in a kind of sarcastic voice.

"I beg your pardon?" Mom sounded confused.

"Thank you," Mrs. Wilson said politely. "That's very thoughtful of you, Mrs. Martin."

"It's not much." Mom sounded apologetic. "I just found out recently how much time my children have been spending here. You're bound to've fed them more than once."

"Oh, I've fed them now and then." Mrs. Wilson chuckled. "That littlest of yours sure has an appetite!"

Mom didn't smile. "I may work seven days a week," she said in a stiff voice, "but I never miss a night sitting down to dinner with my children."

Mrs. Wilson's smile faded. In a voice just as stiff as Mom's, she said, "Ruby, walk Mrs. Martin around back so she can get her children."

Kate scooped up the carrot tops and ran toward the goat pasture. She had heard every word, but she didn't understand what was going on. Why had Mom been so upset with Mrs. Wilson just because she said Chip ate a lot? And why did

Ruby…well, Ruby always had attitude. By now Kate had learned that it didn't always mean she was angry; it was just the way she was. And anyway, if Mom didn't want to deal with a person like Ruby, she shouldn't have come there. After all, the Wilsons were *their* friends, not hers.

Chip and Luther were in the cart, which Billy was pulling nicely toward the opposite side of the pasture. When they reached the fence, Luther flapped the reins. Billy turned back toward the goat shed and took off like a flash.

"Whoa! Whoa!" Luther yelled as the cart bounced wildly over the grass, tipping this way and that.

"Hang on!" Chip shouted.

Kate saw that Billy wasn't going to stop at the shed, but intended to run under it. The shed was high enough for the goat and the cart to go under, but not high enough for the boys, who were standing up in the cart.

"Jump!" Kate yelled.

Chip and Luther leapt from the cart and went rolling across the grass, laughing like maniacs.

Mr. Wilson took the carrot tops from Kate and walked over to the goat shed. "Here, Billy," he called. "Kate brought you a little snack."

Billy snatched a mouthful of carrot tops from Mr. Wilson's hand. When the goat chewed them, they stuck out both sides of his mouth like green whiskers.

"That wasn't so bad for the first time," Mr. Wilson laughed. "A little bit of practice and you boys'll have yourself a first-class harness goat."

Kate started to tell Justin that Mom was here, then saw Mom and Ruby walking across the yard toward them.

"Mrs. Martin, my brother Booker," Ruby said in the same cold voice she used to use on Kate before they became almost-friends. "Booker, you remember Mrs. Martin, who lives down there on the highway?"

Booker grinned at Mom. "How could I forget? Used to walk right by her house to catch the school bus."

"Not the way I remember it." Mom smiled. "Can't count the times I saw that bus coming down the highway, and you up Lost Goat Lane. You'd start running, and I swear you got there first every time. My husband used to say you were the only boy in Florida who could outrun a school bus."

Kate stared at Mom in disbelief. Didn't she realize what she was saying?

Suddenly it seemed that Mom *did* realize what she was saying. She turned very red and stammered, "I beg your pardon, Booker. I guess I ought not—"

Booker interrupted the apology. In a soft voice, the first time Kate had heard him speak in a soft voice, he said, "Just because I can't run anymore, you figure I want folks to forget I ever could?"

Mom looked embarrassed.

"I don't forget things either, Mrs. Martin. Like that time in Atlanta, and what you did for us."

Mom's face turned even redder, but before she had time to answer, Mr. Wilson walked over. "Afternoon, Mrs. Martin. What do you think of my almost-trained goat?"

"Must be as smart as he is handsome," Mom said quickly. "The kids tell me our Sugar's likely to bring us one just like him."

"One or more," Mr. Wilson grinned. "Billy's got a history of siring twins."

"I sure wouldn't complain about that," Mom said.

Chip and Luther galloped up. "What're you doing here, Mom?" Chip demanded. "How come you're not at work?"

"I came to take you home," Mom told him. "Remember I said—"

"Awwww. Do we have to go?" Chip strung the question into one long whine.

"Yes, you do," Mom said firmly. "Booker came to visit his family, and you kids are taking up all his time."

"No problem!" said Booker with a grin that included all of them. "But I have to get something to eat pretty soon or I'll be too weak for the big game tomorrow. You'll all be back for the Big Game, won't you? Around two?"

"What game?" Justin asked.

"Why, our family's traditional Thanksgiving Day, break-a-window baseball work-up." Booker looked from Chip to Kate to Justin. "Of course, we could play without you. But it wouldn't be much of a game with Ruby and Luther and me by ourselves."

"Ruby plays baseball?" Kate asked in surprise. She glanced at Ruby.

"Does Ruby play baseball?" Booker leaned toward Kate. "Why, Ruby could've played pro if it wasn't for one thing."

"What?"

Booker paused dramatically, as if he was about to reveal a big secret. "Fingernails," he said in a loud whisper.

"Fingernails?" they chorused.

"Lethal weapons," Booker said solemnly. "Same as carrying a switchblade. A ball sees nails like that, it just naturally tries to avoid them."

"Oh, Booker!" Ruby grabbed a handful of his tight black curls and gave his head a playful shake. "Get real."

Luther scrambled up into Booker's lap. "Gimme a ride, Uncle Booker. A ride to the house!"

"You bet, pal." Booker glanced up at Ruby. "Good-looking

boy you got here, Sis. Not looking too bad yourself either." He winked at Kate. "Except for the vampire fingernails."

Mom smiled. "Come on, kids. You can come back tomorrow afternoon."

As she pushed them toward the car, Chip yelled at Luther, and Luther at him, like they did every single day, "See you tomorrow!"

# 11

# Mom's Secret Past

Kate sat in the backseat with Justin, looking out at the corn-stalks swishing past. They walked along Lost Goat Lane almost every day but it seemed totally different from the back-seat of her mom's car. But then everything about this after-noon had been strange. First there was Booker not being the way they'd expected him to be, and the bicycle not being a bicycle but part of a goat cart, and that weird conversation between Mom and Mrs. Wilson. Then there was Booker's mysterious remark about Atlanta.

At that moment, as if he had been reading Kate's mind, Justin leaned forward and put his elbows on the back of Mom's seat. "What did Booker mean about Atlanta?"

"Oh, nothing. Your dad and I were in Atlanta once when Booker was in college there," Mom said in a casual voice. "We went to see him play. Chip, get your feet off the dash."

"You took us?" Chip asked.

"You and Kate weren't even born. And Justin wouldn't remember. He was barely walking."

"Did Booker know you were there?" Kate asked.

"We went down to the field between innings," Mom replied. "Justin had to go to the bathroom, so his dad took him. Booker and I…"

Mom stopped at the lane. "Okay, kids. See you later."

They just sat there.

"What, Mom?" Justin asked. "What was it you and Booker did?"

Kate watched Mom's face in the rearview mirror. It had that funny, faraway look again, like she was remembering something that made her feel good. But her hands were gripping the steering wheel tight. She took a deep breath and started talking.

"While I was with Booker down on the field, waiting for Justin and his dad to get back from the bathroom, Booker told me that he was trying to put together an event, him and some of his teammates. He wanted to bring them down here and play an exhibition game to raise money for a scholarship fund."

Mom glanced at Kate out of the corner of her eye. Kate figured that she was getting to the part she didn't want to tell them about. But Mom kept talking.

"Booker said he and his roommate could stay with his folks, but he needed hotel rooms for the rest of the team. Well, there's only one hotel in town and everybody knows how Miss Tutweiler is. If she got wind of the fact that some of the guys were black, and one had a white wife, well, Booker was afraid she'd make up some excuse to keep them out. You know, pretend she was all filled up or something like that. So Booker asked me to reserve the rooms for them."

"What did you tell Miss Tutweiler?" Kate asked.

"I told her I had a bunch of friends coming to town. Booker sent me the money and I paid in advance. I don't know that Miss Tutweiler would've had the nerve to turn away the black ballplayers outright, but the mixed-race couple, well, she would have tried to find a way to keep them out. So I organized a welcoming committee with banners and everything.

With folks waiting at the hotel to greet them, she couldn't act like a throwback there in front of everybody."

Kate laughed. "What did she say?"

"To me? Nothing," Mom said, not laughing at all. "But she had plenty to say to other people."

Kate had an idea of the kind of things Miss Tutweiler might have said to other people about Mom. She'd heard her grandma talking about how it was back in the old days when blacks were fighting for their rights. Kate knew that if a white person had black friends or even stuck up for blacks they got called names worse than the words you saw on the bathroom wall at school. But Miss Tutweiler was a very prim person, even if she was a throwback. Kate couldn't imagine her using words like that.

"I thought all that civil rights stuff was before you were born," Kate said.

Mom sighed. "Well, not exactly. By the time I started school, the civil rights bill had been passed and most places around here were officially integrated. But some people never change. What can I say? It takes most people a long time to learn to trust people who are different from them."

Kate couldn't tell if Mom was just talking about color differences or some other kind of differences. Why, Kate wondered, can't you just get to know a person first and then decide if they're trustworthy, instead of prejudging? But she didn't ask because Mom was looking at her watch.

"Oh no!" Mom exclaimed. "I'm going to be late for work. Come on, kids. Hop out."

Kate and Chip got out, but Justin stood there leaning on the open car door. "Mom," he asked in a puzzled voice. "How come you never got to be friends with the Wilsons? I mean, if you knew Booker?"

"Honey, they live half a mile away. And your dad and I

aren't exactly the same generation as Mr. and Mrs. Wilson." Mom smiled. "When Mrs. Wilson had her hands full with teenagers, I had mine more than full with toddlers. We really don't have a thing in common. Now close the door, son. I've got to go."

Justin slammed the car door and they all waved good-bye. Chip skipped toward the house singing, "Tomorrow, tomorrow. We're going to play ball with Booker. Tomorrow, tomorrow, tomorrow."

Justin grinned at Chip's silly song. Then he turned to Kate. "How about that! Our mom, a civil rights activist!"

Kate frowned. "That was back in Grandma's day."

Justin shrugged. "Yeah. But you heard what Mom said. Even after the laws changed, there were still people who didn't want to give blacks their rights. If Mom helped those ballplayers from Atlanta get their rights in Miss Tutweiler's hotel, that made her an activist."

Kate nodded, but that wasn't the only thing she was confused about. What Mom had said to Justin made it sound like she never wanted to be friends with Mr. and Mrs. Wilson because they were old. Wasn't that prejudging, too? How could Mom know she didn't have anything in common with the Wilsons if she hadn't even taken the trouble to get to know them? Maybe if Mom had tried harder, Ruby would have been more friendly right off.

Then Kate remembered how cold Ruby sounded to Mom on the porch. Maybe Ruby took one look at Mom in her work clothes, holding a paper bag instead of a nicely wrapped present, and thought the same thing about her that she'd thought about Kate the day they came to fetch Sugar: here's some white-trashy person I don't want to have anything to do with.

And why had Mom been so quick to take offense at

Mrs. Wilson's remark about Chip having a big appetite? At home Mom was always nagging Chip to eat more. You'd have thought she'd be glad to hear that when they ate at the Wilsons' he didn't pick at his food!

Kate had always believed that when she got to be thirteen she'd understand grown-ups better, but it seemed that the older she got, the harder it was to figure them out.

# 12

# Playing Ball with Booker

*B*ooker was an amazing pitcher. Leaning sideways in his wheelchair, he'd do a windup that would send the ball over the plate at exactly the level and speed he'd intended, low and slow for the little boys, medium-hard for Kate and Ruby, and downright challenging for Justin. But no matter who was up, when Booker figured that person had had enough time at bat, he'd start laying balls across the plate that were just about unhittable.

They played work-up rules, which meant that when somebody was put out, everybody moved up one position, bypassing the pitcher's position, which Booker kept for himself. Kate, who was up for the third time, made a decent hit, but the ball went straight to Chip on second, who threw it to Luther on first.

"Out!" Luther yelled before Kate's foot touched the base.

Kate took over second base, and everybody moved up one position. It was Ruby's turn to bat. Booker sent a fastball over the plate. Ruby swung but only grazed it.

"Strike one!" Booker intoned.

Booker laid another fastball across the plate, and again Ruby struck at it. The bat connected, but the ball rolled off.

"Foul ball!" Booker yelled.

The next ball was an easy one, but it didn't do Ruby any good. Kate could see that she was already frustrated. Ruby swung too soon and missed completely.

"STRIKE THREEE AND YOU'RE OUT!" Booker roared.

"You could've given me one decent pitch," Ruby grumbled as she passed Booker on her way to second base to take over from Kate, who moved up to first.

"You're blaming me?" Booker rolled his eyes at the others. "It's the fingernails."

Justin stepped up to the plate. Booker narrowed his eyes. Justin narrowed his own eyes. They understood each other perfectly. Everybody saw that Booker wasn't going to fool around. This was serious baseball.

Booker pitched, Justin swung, and the bat connected with a crack. The ball soared all the way to the goat pasture. Justin rounded the bases in a flash and sat down on home plate to wait for Ruby, who had run after the ball.

"Oooh-weee!" Booker exclaimed. "There's a natural-born ballplayer. Reckon you'll be playing on the school team this year, eh, Justin?"

Justin, who had been looking pretty pleased with himself, dropped his shoulders into a slump. Kate knew that look and knew it meant trouble. It was the look Justin got when he brought home a bad report card.

"No point," Justin said, his face turning sullen. "Coach said that unless you have a glove, don't bother."

Kate frowned at Justin, who was staring at the ground. There were actually only three reasons people didn't get picked for the team: if they weren't good enough, didn't have good enough grades, or got into some kind of serious trouble. Justin was certainly good enough and he wasn't in serious trouble, so the only possible reason he'd be kept off the team was bad grades. The bit about the glove was just Justin's way of covering up for the fact that he might not make the team.

Booker must have figured that out, too, because he laughed. "You're jiving me, right, Justin? Telling me your coach is so dumb that if he sees a boy with real good reflexes, a natural hitter, and fast, I mean, *fast*, he's not going to pick that boy for the team just because he doesn't have a glove?" Booker grinned at the others. "Now, I met some dumb coaches in my life, but I never met one that dumb."

Ruby came panting back with the ball. She threw it to Booker and took up her position again on second base. "Have a heart, Justin," she called. "I'm getting too old for long-distance running."

Justin got to his feet and walked over to the plate. Kate saw immediately that he had changed. Instead of wanting to do his best, like before, now he had that old who-cares look on his face. He was going to screw up. She didn't know how, but she knew he would.

Booker pitched again and again. Finally Justin's bat connected. But this time the ball didn't go long-distance. It went in a high arc and came down directly into Ruby's hands. Kate knew that Justin had put the ball exactly where he wanted to. He had put himself out on purpose.

For a minute Booker just stared at Justin, who hadn't even bothered to run for first base. Finally Booker said, "I get it. You're so good you can be in or out, whichever you please."

Since Ruby had caught Justin's fly, that meant they changed places. Just as Ruby picked up the bat, Mrs. Wilson called from the porch, "You-all thirsty? Some ice tea here."

"Thanks, Mama," Booker called back. "Just let me strike this gal out one more time."

Although Booker pretended he was out to get his sister, his pitch was an easy one, and Ruby didn't miss. The ball bounced into the outfield. Justin scooped it up and threw it to first. But Ruby was there ahead of it. She caught the ball and kept running.

"Hey!" yelled Justin.

"No fair!" shouted Luther.

"Catch her!" Kate cried.

Ruby touched second base, third base, and then cut over toward the pitcher. She leapt into Booker's lap and rubbed the ball on his nose.

"Game's over, game's over!" Booker howled. "Gee, Sis, you sure put on some weight!" He pushed her off his lap and called out, "Go on up on the porch, everybody, and get yourselves some tea."

Kate sat down in a rocking chair and quenched her thirst with a long swallow of tea. It might have been the best ice tea she had ever tasted, and this was definitely the best Thanksgiving she could remember.

Booker and Ruby stayed out in the yard for a few minutes talking, then Ruby went into the house. Booker wheeled himself up the ramp onto the porch. Kate had noticed the ramp, which went up to the porch from the side, but had never paid much attention to it. It looked like something Mr. Wilson had built, and now she saw why. It made it possible for Booker to get on and off the porch without anybody helping him.

Chip was sitting next to Luther on the swing. "What happened to your legs, Booker?" he asked.

"Hush up, Chip!" Kate was mortified. Chip knew perfectly well you weren't supposed to mention people's handicaps.

"They got blown off," Booker said, reaching for a glass of ice tea.

"By who?" Chip asked.

"Don't know exactly." Booker squeezed a slice of lemon into his tea. "We were sent in behind enemy lines. The area where we landed was full of land mines, and I stepped on one of them."

"Then what happened?" Chip asked, looking puzzled.

"Well," Booker said slowly, swirling the ice in his tea glass. "I was walking across the sand, point person, in front of my squad. Then all of a sudden, *kerbloom!*"

"Kerbloom?" Chip repeated.

"Next thing I remember was waking up in a hospital with Muzak playing on the intercom. A nurse came in to change the bed, and that's when I noticed I was missing my feet. Plus a good bit of my legs." Booker looked around. "Anybody want more tea?"

Luther and Chip shook their heads no and bounded off the porch. Kate held up her glass for more. "Thank you," she said, her eyes on Booker so as to not miss a word. You never knew what he was going to say next.

Ruby came out of the house and collapsed on the swing. "Can't believe it's Thanksgiving and this hot."

"You stayed too long in that Yankee climate," Booker teased. "Your blood's gone thick."

"Could be."

"How long you been back? Six months?"

"About that."

"Long time for a vacation."

"Don't start on me, Booker!" Ruby's voice was so sharp it made Kate jump.

"Start what?" Booker asked innocently.

"Preaching about what I've got. I know what I've got," Ruby snapped.

"Like what?" Booker challenged. "Give me a fr'instance."

"Fr'instance, legs," Ruby said, kicking the side of his wheelchair. "But that doesn't make me a baseball star."

Kate thought it would be a good idea to change the subject, but she couldn't think of anything to say. Ruby's mouth turned down, giving her the same hopeless expression that Justin often wore.

"You making it doesn't mean everybody can," Ruby grumbled. "There's still a lot of discrimination out there."

"You think I haven't been discriminated against?" Booker demanded.

"Ah, come on, Booker," Ruby snapped back. "There hasn't been any racial discrimination against top athletes in this country since you were born!"

"Yeah," said Booker. His loud voice went real soft. "But what about a top athlete with no feet? You think when I went looking for a coaching job, I didn't face some prejudice because I'm in a wheelchair? But I didn't use that as an excuse for not getting on with my life."

"And I guess not having feet gives you an excuse to go stomping on everybody's feelings!" Ruby yelled, and stormed into the house.

Kate and Justin just sat there, their mouths hanging open. Booker winked at them but Kate was too upset to wink back.

"Time we headed home," Kate mumbled. "I'll go get Chip."

She went to the side of the house and called Chip. He knew it was a go-home call. They had promised Mom they would leave right after the ball game. Chip didn't fool around, but waved good-bye to Luther and ran off down the road toward home.

Kate walked back to the front porch to get Justin. He was at the bottom of the steps, scuffing his toe in the dirt. Kate could tell by the way Booker was looking at him that he was about to give Justin some kind of lecture. She could have told Booker it wouldn't do any good. In Kate's opinion, Justin gave up way too easily, but that's the way he was. Now that he'd made up his mind they were going to have to move pretty soon, he seemed more down on himself than ever.

Kate said, "Bye, Booker. Thanks for letting us play."

"Sure thing," Booker said. Then he looked at Justin. "You know why I didn't make it to the majors?"

"No. Why?"

"I was a real good ballplayer, but I wasn't a hitter. Now you, you're a hitter." Booker took a long swallow of tea, as if giving Justin time to let that sink in. Then he said, "I sure hate to see a player of your caliber not put up a fight to get what he wants."

Justin stood there for a minute, thinking about what Booker said. Then, to Kate's surprise, he stood up straight and stuck out his chest.

"Right," he said with a grin. "Thanks, Booker."

# 13
# Partners

Mom had made such a big deal about not messing up Booker's visit with his family that they didn't go to the Wilsons' the day after Thanksgiving. But on Saturday morning, Kate, Justin, and Chip couldn't stay away any longer. They headed over with some eggs and got to the Wilson house just as Booker was getting in the van to leave.

"Hey, neighbors!" he yelled. "I was hoping I'd get a chance to say good-bye to you all."

"You're leaving already?" Chip asked in a voice full of disappointment.

"That I am," Booker said. "This man's got places to go and people to see."

"What he's got," Ruby said tartly, "is a girlfriend he can't wait to get back to."

Booker looked at the children gathered around. "Now which of you kids told her I had a girlfriend? That was supposed to be a secret."

Luther laughed. "You did, Uncle Booker! You told us!"

Booker reached out the window of the van and flipped Ruby's long braids. "Can't see that you'd mind, Sis. You been picking on me for two days now. I thought you'd be glad to get rid of me."

"Who's been picking on who?" Ruby shot back. "Lucky for you I'm the forgiving type." She was holding four gift-wrapped boxes. As soon as Booker had gotten himself settled in the van, she passed them through the window to him. "Put these right under the air conditioner, and refrigerate them as soon as you get home."

After about a dozen more good-byes from everyone standing around hating to see Booker leave, he gave each one of them a long look, then drove off in a cloud of dust. Kate watched him go and wondered how he'd done that—how he had managed to look at her and Justin and Chip and Luther and Ruby and his mother and father in a way that made it seem like he had a special feeling about each one of them.

"There goes our superstar," Ruby sighed. She put her arm around Mrs. Wilson, who had tears in her eyes.

"I brought some duck eggs," Kate said. "You want me to put them in the kitchen?"

"Sure, Katie," Mrs. Wilson said. "Come on in."

"You boys come with me," Mr. Wilson said, heading around the house toward the goat pasture. "You're going to be surprised how much old Billy has learned about cart-pulling."

What surprised Kate was the Wilsons' living room. Instead of its normal neatness, she saw piles of small white boxes, gold ribbon, craft materials, and other decorative stuff. Ruby sat down at the desk, picked up one of the boxes, and began to write on it with a fancy fountain pen.

"What do you think of that?" she asked, handing Kate the box.

Across the top, Ruby had written "Ruby's Exquisite Handmade Chocolates" in gold ink with lots of fancy curlicues.

"Wow!" Kate exclaimed. "I didn't know you knew how to do calligraphy."

"One of my many talents," Ruby said, tossing her braids.

Kate handed the little box back, carefully so as to not smear the gold ink, and went into the kitchen to put away the duck eggs.

"Just set them there in the refrigerator," Mrs. Wilson told her. She looked tired. Kate could see why. The kitchen was a mess. The sink was stacked with dirty pots, pans, bowls, spoons, and knives. The smell of chocolate was overpowering. There were splotches of burned chocolate on the stove, and smears of chocolate on the cupboard doors, the counter, the fridge, and the floor.

Kate picked up a sponge and started scrubbing the chocolate off the stove. Mrs. Wilson glanced up from the sink where she was washing dishes and smiled. "Thank you, Katie," she said. When Kate finished the stove, she cleaned chocolate fingerprints off the cupboard door, then wiped the counter, the fridge, the floor, and the wastebasket. "You are one good worker, Katie Martin. Why don't you go out and see if Ruby needs any help?"

Kate washed her hands and went back into the living room to watch Ruby. "Want some help?"

"Well..." Ruby didn't sound enthusiastic about having a helper. Then she seemed to change her mind. "Maybe." She picked up one of the little white boxes. "See here? I'm gluing a gold bow on each box, and I want one of these plastic rubies glued in the exact center of each bow. Can you do that?"

"Sure!" Kate was thrilled that Ruby would trust her with such an artistic assignment. "What're all these boxes for?"

"Samples." Ruby stopped writing and lowered her voice. "What happened, see, was Booker kept ragging on me about not doing anything with my life till I was ready to strangle him. Then I had this idea. Friday morning I got him to take me to town, where I bought all the ingredients to make fancy chocolates like the ones we made in the gourmet candy shop where I used to work in New York. I spent all the rest of the day and most of last night making candy, and *voilà!*"

"Is that what you gave Booker to take with him?" Kate asked.

"Yeah. He bought the first four pounds for his girlfriend and her mom and a couple more friends. The rest I used for these samples." Ruby waved her hand at the little boxes. "There are four pieces in each box. My plan is to take them into town this afternoon and leave one for each of the shop-keepers on Main Street. Then go back next week for orders." Ruby gave Kate a brilliant smile. "Which I know I can get."

"Oh, Ruby, you are so smart! I would never have thought of something like that!"

Ruby went into the kitchen and came back with a piece of candy. "Open up," she said, and popped it into Kate's mouth.

"Umm!" Kate said. The center of the candy had an almondy crunch, and the chocolate on the outside was smooth and but-tery. When she'd sucked the last bit of the flavor out of her mouth, she said, "That's the best candy I ever tasted!"

"It's going to be the best anybody around here's ever tasted," Ruby said confidently. She picked up her special cal-ligraphy pen and studied the point for a minute. Then she said the last thing in the world Kate would have expected her to say.

"Maybe," Ruby drawled, "I could use a partner."

"You mean—" Kate was about to say, "me?" but she was sure Ruby didn't mean that. Ruby was nice to her almost all the time now, but it was mostly in a helpful way, suggestions about how to fix her hair or reminding her to stand up straight. She never got the feeling that Ruby actually liked her.

"Meaning you," Ruby said, arching an eyebrow at her. "Unless you have something better to do."

"No! I mean yes! I mean… Oh, Ruby, I'd love to be your partner. Just tell me what to do."

"Well, for starters, you can help me take these samples around to the shops this afternoon. A little town like this, I expect you know most people."

"Oh sure. In this town, everybody knows everybody."

"I remember," said Ruby. "And knows everybody's business, too."

It was two in the afternoon when they started out. Ruby noticed Mom's car at the house when they passed the end of their lane. "You want to let your mom know you're going to town?" she asked.

Kate hesitated, then said, "No need. I told Justin."

What she had actually told Justin was to tell Mom that she had walked to town to pick up more library books. Kate knew Mom wouldn't mind that, but she had some doubts about what she would say about going to town with Ruby. Given how almost-rude Ruby had been to her the day before Thanksgiving, Mom might think up some excuse for Kate not to go. But she never objected to her kids going to the library. And it wasn't a lie. They'd pass right by the library coming into town. Kate could stop there for a minute on the way home.

It took almost an hour to walk to town. The land around was flat as a pancake. Some fields were planted in corn, some in beans, and some in other vegetables, because this part of Florida was the winter vegetable–growing capital of the country. Fortunately there were Australian pines along the highway, and they gave a little shade on the footpath. Kate was glad for the shade because although the chocolates were packed against bags of ice to keep them cool, it didn't help keep her cool. In fact, the ice only made the little baskets she and Ruby carried that much heavier. By the time they got to the town line sign, Kate was sweating and her arms were aching.

"Population 3075," Ruby read the sign and laughed. "That's about how many people live in one square block of Manhattan." She looked down Main Street, which more or less started at the library and went on for about a mile, all the way out to the hospital and the feed store and a farm equipment place. Main Street went that far but the town didn't. What everybody called "downtown" only went from the library at this end to the bank three blocks down. Most of the town's stores were crammed in between, on both sides of the street, except for a few things like the beauty parlor and movie theater and video rental place, which were up side streets.

"Tired?" Ruby asked.

"A little," Kate admitted.

"Me, too," Ruby said. "But just you wait. Once folks around here get a taste of my chocolates, they'll be coming to *us*." She walked gaily into a kitchenware shop, which also sold some hardware items and rented carpet shampooers.

A man who was putting up Christmas decorations glanced over his shoulder. "Sorry, no peddlers," he said.

"We're not—"

"We don't need anything," he interrupted, climbing down off his stepladder. When he turned around, Kate saw that the fly of his pants was unzipped. Before she could look away, he reached down and yanked up the zipper. He glared at them so hard, they backed out the door in a hurry.

"That wasn't the kind of place for my product anyway," Ruby said. With a determined look, she headed for the place next door, a small café. Kate was glad to see that the cashier in the café was Mrs. Sikes, the mother of a girl in her class.

"Good morning, ma'am. My name's Ruby Wilson. I—"

"Sorry, we're busy," Mrs. Sikes said. "Can't talk to you now."

Kate looked around. There was only one man at the counter, all the way down at the end, drinking coffee.

"I have a gift for the owner," Ruby said coolly.

"She's not in," Mrs. Sikes snapped.

"I'll just leave it," Ruby said. "And my card. You will give it to her?"

Mrs. Sikes acted as if Ruby had asked her to do some major favor. She screwed up her face like she was about to say no.

Kate stepped quickly up to the cash register. "Thanks, Mrs. Sikes. Say hi to Billy Sue for me."

In fact, Kate hated Billy Sue Sikes, who was one of the biggest bullies in school. But she figured that if Mrs. Sikes knew they were in the same class, she'd think they were friends and wouldn't have such a bad attitude toward Ruby.

Mrs. Sikes gave Kate a surprised look, as if noticing her for the first time. "Yeah," she said. "Oh sure. I will." She looked down at the pretty sample box. "And I'll give this to the boss."

Ruby and Kate continued up the street, stopping at all the stores they thought might be interested in ordering some. Once Ruby explained she was only giving out samples, most of the clerks agreed to take a box. It only took about twenty minutes to walk from one end of downtown to the other. They finished one side and started back down the other.

Ruby pointed to a little gift shop just around the corner from the ice cream store. "Who runs that place?"

"Old Mr. Bainbridge used to, but he died. Now it's his son, Mr. Bainbridge Jr. Everybody calls him Mr. Junior. He looks old for a junior, but Mama says that's just because he drinks so much."

Ruby laughed. "Okay, let's say hello to Mr. Junior."

Mr. Junior was squatted down behind the counter. When they pushed open the door he stood up quickly.

"How can I help you ladies?" he asked with a smile. He slid his liquor bottle behind a display.

Ruby put one of the boxes on the counter and smiled back at him. "I'm selling homemade chocolates. We've brought you a sample."

"Oh, I'm not a candy eater," Mr. Junior began. Then, seeing the disappointed look on Kate's face, he said, "But my mother adores chocolates. Reckon I could give it to her. Here—" He reached into his pocket and brought out a crumpled dollar bill.

"Oh no," Ruby explained. "This I brought today is free. If you want to order more—"

"Nothing in life is free, missy." Mr. Junior grabbed Ruby's hand and pressed the dollar into it. "Now you and the little girl run along, and have a nice day, hear?"

Kate took one look at Ruby's face and saw that she had better get her out of there, fast. Kate knew that Mr. Junior was just trying to be nice, but Ruby didn't seem to be taking that into consideration. They were barely back on the sidewalk before Ruby exploded.

"That condescending old wino! People around here got their minds squinched shut so tight you couldn't shove a dime in edgewise." She was talking so loud that a woman passing by turned to stare. Ruby flopped down on a bench outside the ice cream store and glared at the woman.

Kate sighed. It was hard dealing with Ruby's mood swings.

"I'm going over there to the bathroom," Kate said, pointing to Ralph's Gas-and-Go. She eased away, figuring it was a good idea to give Ruby a little time by herself to cool off.

# Partners

There were two guys hanging around the gas pumps and another one changing oil on a car. They didn't notice Kate when she went past them to the bathroom. She sort of knew them, or at least knew their names. José was the mechanic who had put the new battery in Mom's car last summer. Ralph was the chubby one who owned the station. Then there was Bubba, a big black guy who hung around there a lot, polishing his big black motorcycle. Most of the time, including today, he wore a white T-shirt that said, "Harley Power is Black Power."

On her way out of the bathroom Kate stopped at the water-cooler for a drink. The guys still didn't notice her because they were staring at Ruby, who was crossing the street toward the station. Ruby had the kind of looks that always turned heads. Kate could see that what got people's attention wasn't so much Ruby's classy jeans and polished boots, but the way she marched along posture-perfect, head held high and long beaded braids swinging.

"Reckon I'll go get me some of that action." Bubba grinned at his buddies.

Ralph laughed. "Bubba Lee, if you ain't got the flappinest mouth I ever heard! You come within three feet of that woman, she'll be hitting at you with a flyswatter." He swatted at Bubba's back with a greasy rag.

José looked up from the car he was working on. "Honey like that's looking for a man, hombre. One with a job. Which you don't exactly have."

"You don't know nothing, man. She's coming right over here." Bubba patted his motorcycle. "Me and this machine, we're mag-netic."

"Man, when's the last time you looked in the mirror?" Ralph scoffed. "What you got that a woman like that might be wantin'?"

"Something neither of you chumps got." Bubba gunned the motorcycle. "Trans-por-*tay*-shun."

Kate stood by the watercooler feeling totally invisible. But Ruby saw her and instead of continuing across the street, made an impatient motion for Kate to come there. Kate ran to her. She wanted to tell Ruby about what the guys had said, but before she could open her mouth, Ruby snapped, "Let's go home."

Kate looked into Ruby's basket. "You've got one sample left. We ought to give it to somebody."

"Like who?" Ruby said irritably. "I've just about had it." She glanced up the street. "There's the hotel. Didn't it used to have a gift shop? You know who runs it?"

"Yes," Kate said hesitantly. "Miss Tutweiler."

"That old biddy? I'd have thought she'd dried up and blown away by now."

"Oh no. She's very active in, well, in just about every-thing." Kate stood there thinking about Miss Tutweiler and whether it was a good idea to go there with Ruby, consider-ing that Ruby had one kind of attitude and Miss Tutweiler had another. If either of them showed too much attitude, that could be a problem.

But Kate was also thinking about something else. "Miss Tutweiler goes to the same church as us," she told Ruby. "She loves sweets. At church socials, I've seen her take three desserts on her plate at one time."

"Hmph" was all Ruby said.

Kate saw that Ruby didn't understand. "You know how some people can't keep from taking more even when it's not polite? That's how Miss Tutweiler is. I bet if you opened a box of candy in front of her, even if she was saying no-thank-you, she'd be grabbing a piece before she could stop herself."

Ruby stood there a minute. She seemed to be considering what Kate had said. The guys at the gas station were still clowning around trying to get her attention, but as far as Kate could tell Ruby was ignoring them.

"All right," Ruby decided suddenly. "Let's give the old hog a chance."

Kate liked Miss Tutweiler's hotel. It had a patio dining area that was especially nice in the summertime. Mom used to take Kate, Justin, and Chip there sometimes for an ice cream sundae or a banana split. But now Mom said they couldn't afford it.

Miss Tutweiler was behind the cash register, which was located so that nobody could pass through the hotel lobby or the dining room without her seeing them. She had white hair and wore a white suit, plus makeup about an inch thick.

Kate knew how Miss Tutweiler felt about black people. She had heard her at church talking about how wonderful the "coloreds" were who used to work for her family. She always added that times sure had changed, in a tone of voice that let you know that she, for one, did not approve of the changes.

Among the people having lunch in the patio was one black man. He was Mr. Jackson, the new high school math teacher. Kate was pretty sure that his having lunch here was one of the changes that Miss Tutweiler didn't like. Miss Tutweiler hadn't seen Ruby yet, but when she did, she probably wasn't going to like that either, not with Ruby holding her head so high and not smiling even a little. In this town, even if you didn't like somebody, you smiled. Otherwise people thought you were stuck-up.

Kate stepped quickly to the cash register ahead of Ruby and said, "Good afternoon, Miss Tutweiler."

"Good afternoon, Katie." Miss Tutweiler looked Kate up and down. For one awful second Kate thought she was going to make some remark about her coming to town dressed in cutoffs and a T-shirt. Miss Tutweiler only smiled sadly and said, "How's your mama, dear?"

"Fine, Miss Tutweiler, ma'am," Kate said in her most polite voice. "This is my friend Ruby."

Ruby stripped the bow off the last box of samples, lifted the lid, and held it out to Miss Tutweiler. Ruby held the box high and close, so Miss Tutweiler couldn't help but smell the candy.

"Hand-dipped chocolates," Ruby urged. "Go ahead, have one."

Miss Tutweiler looked startled. "No thank you. I—" Her powdered nose twitched slightly.

"They're true gourmet chocolates," Ruby added. "The kind you'd normally find only in the very finest New York shops."

Miss Tutweiler's fingertips moved upward, toward the box. "Well, maybe one," she murmured.

Miss Tutweiler nibbled at the chocolate, then, with a little moan, pushed the whole thing into her mouth. "Mmmm."

Ruby set the box next to the cash register. "This is just a sample. For you, ma'am. Though I am taking orders."

Miss Tutweiler's fingers were already inching out for a second piece. "It is very good," she admitted. She stuffed the candy into her mouth and looked over the counter at Kate's ragged tennis shoes. Then she said briskly to Ruby, "How much is it?"

"The sample is free," Ruby said patiently. "But if you'd like to order more, here's my card. The prices are listed on the back. It's a traditional Swiss recipe. I use only the very finest ingredients."

Kate noticed that Mr. Jackson had come up and was waiting behind them to pay his check. She nudged Ruby and they stepped aside so he could get to the cash register.

"Excellent lunch," he said, giving Miss Tutweiler a big smile. He handed over the money and then reached right into Miss Tutweiler's sample box, took one of the chocolates, and popped it into his mouth.

"Mmmm! No cheap after-dinner mints for your customers, eh? Leave it to you, Miss Tutweiler, to add the quality touch."

"Why, of course, Mr. Jackson," Miss Tutweiler said, looking annoyed and pleased at the same time. "That's how I was brought up."

"Hospitality in the finest Southern tradition," he said, spilling another big smile all over her. "Thank you again for the lovely lunch." As he turned to go he winked at Kate, but he didn't once look at Ruby, which was pretty surprising, since just about everybody looked at Ruby. Kate noticed that Ruby hadn't looked at him either. Still, she had a feeling that they had definitely checked each other out.

Miss Tutweiler studied the card Ruby had given her. "I'll take three one-pound boxes," she said briskly. "If they sell, I'll order more. When can you deliver them?"

"Uh, next Saturday," Ruby said, and actually smiled.

"Very good. I'll expect you on Saturday."

As they turned away, Miss Tutweiler added, "I do like to see girls like you trying to get ahead."

# 14
# Trouble on Wheels

O ut on the sidewalk Kate looked up at Ruby, expecting to see the smile still on her face. Instead, Ruby looked furious. She walked so fast that Kate had to trot to keep up with her.

"What are you mad about?" Kate asked. "She gave us an order!"

"Charity," Ruby exploded. "Sugar-coated charity from that gluttonous old biddy. A person can go to hell for gluttony, you know. I hope she does! Her and all this town's close-minded—"

They stopped at an intersection. Ruby's voice was drowned out by the roar of a motorcycle. Bubba Lee pulled up in front of them, blocking the crosswalk. He grinned at Ruby.

"You wasn't baby-sittin', I'd give you a lift. Save you wearing out them pretty boots on the hard pavement."

"Get that thing out of my way!" Ruby snapped. She tried to walk in front of the motorcycle.

Bubba pulled forward, blocking her path. "Thirty minutes and we could be in Palm Beach."

Ruby grabbed Kate's hand and practically dragged her behind the motorcycle and across the street against the light.

Bubba circled around and pulled alongside them on the

Trouble on Wheels

other side of the street, in front of the root beer stand. Still grinning, he asked, "How about a root beer?"

When Ruby didn't answer, he looked at Kate. "What about you, little sister? Sun's mighty hot today. You want something to drink?"

Kate gave Ruby a questioning look. She really was thirsty, and she couldn't think of anything she'd rather have right then than an ice-cold root beer. But she didn't want to make Ruby more upset than she already was.

"Well?" Ruby asked sharply. "Do you want something to drink?"

"Uh, yeah. If you do," Kate answered uncertainly.

Ruby turned a sharp left and walked across the parking lot toward the root beer stand. Kate trotted beside her.

Bubba roared his bike up to the window ahead of them. "Three root beers," he yelled at the clerk.

The clerk filled two frosty mugs with foamy root beer and shoved them through the window. Bubba handed one to Ruby and one to Kate. Kate wondered why he didn't fill three mugs and pass them through all at once, the way he did when Mom ordered three for her and Justin and Chip. The clerk not only didn't set one out for Bubba, but he turned away and started washing dirty mugs, like he didn't see Bubba standing there.

Bubba put his head halfway in the window and yelled, "How about one more, buddy?"

"Ain't your buddy," the clerk mumbled into the sink, and washed another couple of mugs before he finally turned around and filled one—not a cold one but one hot out of the dishwater—for Bubba.

"Four dollars thirty-three cents," he said sourly.

Bubba didn't say anything about not getting a frosty mug. He slowly took out his wallet, slowly opened it, and slowly pulled out a wad of bills. In fact, he took almost as much time handing a twenty-dollar bill to the clerk as the clerk had taken handing him his root beer.

The clerk flipped greasy blond hair back from his forehead and stared at the twenty-dollar bill. "Got anything smaller?" he asked.

"Nope." Bubba waited for his change, then put the bills back in the wad and shoved it in his pocket.

It was the most money Kate had ever seen, but Ruby didn't seem to notice. She didn't pay much attention to Bubba either, not even bothering to say "thank you" for the root beers.

Bubba slurped his drink. "Where you gals headed?"

Ruby didn't answer, so Kate said, "We're just on our way home."

"And where's home?" Bubba asked.

"On Lost Goat Lane." Kate pointed down the highway they'd walked in on. "It's about three miles thataway."

Bubba looked past Kate to Ruby, who was standing behind her. "Sure you wouldn't druther take a spin out to Palm Beach?"

Ruby didn't answer. Kate thought it wasn't polite to drink the root beer Bubba bought for them and not talk to him, so she said, "Bet it'd be fun to go to Palm Beach on a motorcycle."

Bubba grinned at her in a teasing way. "Get yourself growed up some, little sister, and I might think about it."

Kate heard the clerk make a snorting noise. She glanced at him. He had his eyes narrowed, watching her in a really mean way.

"If you want a ride home, Kate, just say so," Ruby said sharply.

Kate almost choked on the last sip of her root beer. Ruby's moods were changing so fast she couldn't keep up with them. "I don't know," she said. "I mean, I never rode on a motorcycle before."

"Up to you," Ruby said.

# Trouble on Wheels

Kate looked at the shining motorcycle. The black gas tank was so polished you could see your reflection in it. The seat behind Bubba was big and padded. Kate took a step toward the bike and stopped, scared. Then she flung one leg over the seat and slipped on behind Bubba. Ruby slid on behind her. Kate leaned over to set her empty root beer mug on the counter next to Ruby's, which was still half-full. The clerk said a word Kate couldn't make out, but from the way his lip curled at her and from the way he jerked his head at Bubba, she knew it was about her being with him. And she knew it was not a nice word.

Bubba gunned the engine. Ruby wrapped her arms around Kate's waist and yelled, "Hold on!"

Kate grabbed Bubba's waist and held on. As they drove past the side of the root beer stand, a door opened and somebody flung out a pan of hot water. Most of it went on the ground, but some of it splashed on Ruby's boot and Kate's leg.

"Ow!" Kate yelled, more surprised than hurt.

Ruby jerked her wet boot up in the air. Bubba pulled the bike to the side of the road and, holding the handlebars with one hand, he yanked a bandanna out of his pocket and wiped Ruby's boot. Then he stuck the bandanna back in his pocket, grabbed the handlebars with both hands, and roared away, all of them laughing like fools.

In one minute they were out of town sailing along the highway. Kate, snug between Bubba and Ruby, felt both protected and free as a bird. It had taken her and Ruby almost an hour to walk to town this morning. They'd be home in a few minutes. Kate wished they'd never get there. She closed her eyes and imagined they were on their way to Palm Beach. She pretended that when she opened her eyes she'd see waves curling out of a blue ocean and crashing on a long sandy beach shaded by green palm trees.

What she saw, when she opened her eyes, was Mom's car. Kate's stomach did a flip-flop. Mom had never told her not to ride on a motorcycle, but, well, some things you didn't need to be told. Some things you just knew your mother would never in a million years let you do. And if you did them without asking and your mother found out, you'd be in serious trouble.

But Bubba was driving fast, and Mom was going the opposite way. Maybe Mom hadn't seen her. After all, Kate was behind Bubba, who was a pretty big guy.

"It's that dirt road up there. Go right," Kate yelled, although right was the only direction you could go, since on the other side of the highway was nothing but the trail leading to the big canal.

"Hang on," Bubba yelled back.

Ruby's arms squeezed Kate's waist and Kate clung tight to Bubba as he turned off the highway onto Lost Goat Lane.

"About half a mile down," Ruby yelled.

They bumped down the dusty road faster than Kate ever had before. She hoped there were no turtles crossing, because if one got in the way, it didn't stand a chance.

Bubba roared into the Wilsons' front yard. For an instant Kate thought he was going to drive the motorcycle right up Booker's wheelchair ramp onto the porch. But he stopped at the bottom of the ramp and sat there racing the engine. The noise seemed to hit the side of the house and bounce back at them twice as loud.

Mrs. Wilson rushed out onto the porch. "What on earth?"

When she saw Kate and Ruby getting off the bike, her expression turned to outrage. "Ruby Wilson, you got no better sense than to put that child on the back of a motorcycle?" she shouted down at her daughter.

Ruby looked embarrassed, and Kate felt herself flush. How

awful of Mrs. Wilson to scold Ruby as if she were a child, especially in front of a guy! Not that Bubba seemed to mind. He just sat there on his big black Harley, grinning at Ruby like he thought she was the prettiest woman he'd ever seen—which she probably was.

"Oh, Mama, we just—"

Mr. Wilson appeared from the side of the house. "What's going on?" he asked loudly.

Ruby took a deep breath. "Not a thing, Papa. Bubba here just gave us a two-minute ride and—"

"In two minutes you've wiped out the respect I spent fifty years building!" Mrs. Wilson shouted.

Kate was dumbfounded. She had never heard Mrs. Wilson raise her voice, and couldn't believe she could get this angry.

Luther came out onto the porch. "Mama," he called. "There's a lady on the phone. She said she asked for three boxes of candy and now she wants six."

"Take a message," Ruby snapped. "Come on," she said to Kate. "We got work to do."

"You see what I mean?" Mrs. Wilson cried, pointing up the road. A car was approaching in a storm cloud of dust. Kate didn't need to be told who it was.

Mom spun a U-turn, stopped in front of the house, and jumped out of the car. "Get in the car, Kate," she said in a voice that made Kate's stomach do a double flip-flop.

"But Mom, Ruby and me—"

Mrs. Wilson came down the steps. "Mrs. Martin, I am awfully sorry."

Mom interrupted in a tight, furious voice. "I'm sorry, too, Mrs. Wilson. I would've thought my daughter had better sense, even if yours doesn't!"

Ruby, who had already started up the steps, came back

down and leaned against the motorcycle. "Go ahead, Mama. 'Pologize to that white lady," she said in an exaggerated drawl.

"Well, I *do* apologize," Mrs. Wilson said sharply. "I am very sorry that my daughter's lacking common sense. And Mrs. Martin, I'm sorry that you're so lacking common courtesy that you could come up in my yard like this and start in on me and my family! Why, we...we got better things to do!"

Kate's mother looked like she'd been slapped in the face. "Well, I never! You people—"

Ruby started toward Mom, her fists clenched. "Nobody stands on our property and mouths off about 'you people'!"

Mom gasped and backed toward the car. "You're not going to town with Ruby again, Kate! Get in the car right now!"

"Mom, are you crazy?" Kate yelled from the front seat. "I *am* in the car!"

Mom jumped in and tried to take off so fast she killed the engine.

Mr. Wilson glowered at Bubba. "Take that noisy thing and get outta here, boy. You'll be upsetting my goats so they don't give a pint of milk tonight."

"Yes sir," Bubba said with a big grin.

Mom got the car restarted, but before she could pull away, Bubba zoomed past. Ruby was on the motorcycle behind him.

Kate heard Luther scream. She looked back. Mrs. Wilson was holding onto Luther to keep him from running after the motorcycle. His arms were stretched out in the direction his mother had gone and he was sobbing as if his heart would break.

Kate couldn't tell for sure, but from the expressions on Mr. and Mrs. Wilsons' faces, it looked like they might be crying, too.

# 15
# Ugly Old Motorcycle

Mom was either too mad or in too much of a hurry to get to work to talk to Kate. When she stopped to let Kate out of the car, all she said was, "Don't you dare step one foot off this place till I get back!"

Kate trudged to the house and holed up in her room.

A few minutes later Justin came in. "Whew! Hot in here," he said.

"Well, I might as well get used to it," Kate mumbled. "I'm probably grounded for life."

"What happened?" he asked.

"Nothing."

Justin stood there for a minute, jiggling his baseball. Then he asked, "Did it have anything to do with that motorcycle that just went by?"

"Yeah," Kate answered. "I came home on it."

"You're kidding! That must've been fun."

"It was. For about three seconds. Then everybody went crazy. Mrs. Wilson started yelling at Ruby and Mr. Wilson was yelling at this guy Bubba who brought us home and Mom came and started yelling at me and Ruby yelled at Mom. Then Ruby got back on Bubba's bike and took off with him to Palm Beach and left Luther screaming after her like a two-year-old."

"Bubba Lee?" Justin lifted his eyebrows. "What were you doing with him? They say he and Ralph sell crack."

"So you think he slipped some into my root beer?" Kate said sarcastically. "Mom's the one who went berserk, not me. All that happened was he gave us a ride home. It was just so hot and…"

Kate choked up and she stopped trying to explain. After a minute Justin left her alone. She lay on the bed staring at the ceiling as tears dripped out the corners of her eyes and slid down the sides of her face.

***

When she woke up, Justin was standing there with a pail of goat milk. "I did your chores for you," he said. "Supper's almost ready. Mom'll be home pretty soon."

"Thanks," Kate said. "Did Sugar give you any trouble?"

"She wasn't too happy to see me, but once she had her grain she behaved pretty well. Except when I first sat down to milk her. She gave me a little nip to show that she knew I wasn't you." Justin held out his arm to show the teeth prints where Sugar had bit him. "Didn't break the skin, though."

Kate took the pail of milk and carried it out to the kitchen.

"Where's Chip?" she asked. She strained the milk and put it in the fridge. Through the window she saw Chip walking slowly up the driveway. He was scuffing his feet and looking unhappy. "Oh, there he is. Where's he been?"

"I don't know," Justin said. "I guess over at the Wilsons'."

"No," Kate said. "he came from the other direction."

Once again it crossed her mind that Chip might have gone to the big canal alone, but it didn't seem likely now that he knew for a fact the big alligator was a killer. She was going to ask him where he'd been, but he didn't come into the house right away. Instead, he went to feed the ducks and collect the eggs. Then Mom drove up and Chip came into the house with her. Kate didn't want to ask where he'd been in front of Mom, in case it was somewhere he wasn't supposed to go. No need to make Mom madder than she already was.

Kate suffered through a silent dinner. Nobody was smiling and nobody was hungry. Justin took only half as much food as usual. Mom pretended to eat, but Kate didn't even try. Chip poked at his beans with his fork, pushing them from one side of his plate to another. Kate figured Chip was thinking about Go-Boy. She wished Go-Boy was under the table like he used to be, too, waiting to eat whatever Chip didn't want.

Finally Mom looked at Chip. "You haven't had your bath yet."

"I'll do it now." Chip jumped up from the table and scooted into the bathroom before Mom could scold him about not finishing his food.

Mom said, "Kate, I want to talk to you about Ruby."

Kate had been holding in her feelings all afternoon, holding in until she felt like she would explode. And explode is what she did. "It wasn't Ruby who wanted to go on the motorcycle!" she yelled. "It was me. You never said I couldn't!"

"It's not just the motorcycle," Mom said quietly.

Kate jumped up from the table. She started running dishwater and clattering plates into the sink, making a lot of noise. She didn't want to hear what she knew Mom was about to say.

Mom raised her voice. "I just don't want you hanging around with—"

"Fine!" Kate shouted. "You don't want me going down to the Wilsons', fine! Candy business is over. We won't even fill the orders we got now!"

One of the plates slipped out of her hand and broke. Kate flung the pieces into the wastebasket and shrieked, "I hated that ugly old motorcycle anyway!"

Mom sat there not saying a word. She didn't even scold Kate for breaking the plate. Instead, she stood up, went outside, and got into the car. Kate watched the car go up the driveway and turn down Lost Goat Lane toward the Wilsons' place. Mom was probably going back to fight with the Wilsons some more. Anything that wasn't already ruined, she was probably going to ruin now. Tears puddled in Kate's eyes and dripped down into the dishwater.

Justin pushed her away from the sink. "Why don't you go in your room to bawl? I'll do the dishes tonight."

\*\*\*

Mom was gone about an hour. By the time she got back, Kate had her pajamas on and was in bed. When Mom peeked into her room, she pretended to be asleep. But Mom walked in, switched on the lamp, and sat down on the side of Kate's bed.

"You don't have to talk to me," her mother said. "But I have some things to say and you do have to listen."

Kate wanted to put her hands over her ears, but she didn't dare. She threw her arm over her eyes instead, as if the light was bothering them.

"I just went to see the Wilsons. They're pretty upset. Ruby's still out with Bubba Lee, and he's not the nicest boy in town. I don't think he's the kind of person they want their daughter running around with. And I *know* he's not the kind of person I want my daughter running around with."

There was a long silence. Then Mom said, "The reason I went down there tonight was to apologize. I had no right to blame Ruby. You are old enough to know that you should not have accepted a ride on anybody's motorcycle."

Mom was silent again. When she spoke it was in a strange, quiet voice, as if she was talking to herself.

"I always imagined how much fun we'd have when you got to this age. I wanted to teach you how to design your own clothes, and go to movies with you, sometimes without the boys, just the two of us, and afterwards go somewhere for ice cream sundaes and, you know, girl talk." Mom paused. "But the way things have turned out, with me working all the time, we have hardly any time together. And you're growing up," she whispered. "So fast."

Again Mom fell silent. She was quiet so long that Kate opened her eyes a crack to see her face. There were tears on Mom's cheeks.

Kate didn't care how Mom felt. She wasn't going to feel sorry for her, and she wasn't going to feel ashamed of herself for a two-minute ride on a motorcycle, which, while it lasted, was fun.

But Mom didn't seem to be thinking about the motorcycle. She stroked Kate's hair back from her forehead in an absent-minded way. When she got around to talking again, it turned out she'd been thinking about the Wilsons. "They were on the front porch. Mrs. Wilson seemed really hostile at first. Then Mr. Wilson went in and got some ice tea and invited me to sit down. We got to talking, me about how it worries me that I'm not spending enough time with you kids, and Mrs. Wilson about how she stayed home all the time when Ruby was growing up but that didn't stop Ruby from running away. She said it seems like the smaller a family gets, the harder it is to hold together what's left. Mr. Wilson said he reckons all of you kids are suffering from not having fathers, which is why it's so nice for everybody when Booker comes home." Mom let out a long sigh. "I can't be both mom and dad to you kids, Katie. I would if I could, but some things one parent just can't do."

Kate knew that if she kept quiet, pretty soon Mom would stop talking. And sure enough, she gave up. Kate turned over so her face was to the wall. Mom leaned down and kissed her on the cheek, then went out of the room.

The Wilsons had their problems and Mom had hers and Kate had hers. Kate's problem was that the only friend she had was Ruby. Even though it was a pretty one-sided friendship, it was better than nothing. But just when they'd started working together and it looked like Ruby might start liking her instead of just putting up with her, Mom was going to mess it up by forbidding her to do anything with Ruby.

Maybe Mom wouldn't even have to forbid her, because maybe Ruby wouldn't come back. Luther had screamed like he thought his mother was leaving forever. Maybe she was. Kate curled up in a ball and pulled the covers tight around her shoulders. Maybe Ruby had run away for good with Bubba Lee on that ugly old motorcycle.

# 16

# Work, Not Fun

Kate stayed awake a long time, listening for the motorcycle to pass by. She finally fell asleep. If Ruby came home, Kate didn't hear the motorcycle bringing her. When she woke up it was late morning, which was okay, since it was Sunday. Mom had already gone to work, but she'd left a note saying that she and the Wilsons had agreed that it would be a good idea for Kate and Ruby to continue their candy-making. People should finish what they'd started, the note said. So after the morning chores, Kate, Chip, and Justin walked down to the Wilsons'. Kate was worried. What if Ruby still wasn't back?

When they got to the house, Justin went around back to the workshop to see what Mr. Wilson was doing. Chip went with him, probably expecting Luther to be there, too. But when Kate went up on the porch and looked through the screen door, she saw Luther sitting on the couch next to Mrs. Wilson. She was reading to him from *The Jungle Book*.

"Baloo taught him the Wood and Water Laws, how to speak politely to the wild bees and how to warn the water snakes in the pools before he splashed down among them," Mrs. Wilson read.

"Now the animals won't hurt him, huh?" Luther asked.

"Animals are just like people, honey. Most of them won't bother you if you don't bother them. Only now and then you run into one that's dangerous. You have to use a little common sense."

Mrs. Wilson looked up and saw Kate. "Come on in, honey. Ruby's not waked up yet, but you can go on in the kitchen and get started if you want. I'll tell her you're here." To Luther she said, "I bet Chip's around back. Why don't you go out and show him how good you can drive old Billy now?"

Luther went out through the kitchen. Mrs. Wilson went down the hall calling, "Ruby!"

There was no answer. For one terrible minute, Kate thought that Ruby wasn't there—that Mrs. Wilson just thought she'd come home but she really hadn't.

Then Mrs. Wilson spoke again, much louder. "You get your head out from under that pillow, girl! This is your *mama* speaking to you!"

"What time is it?" Kate heard Ruby ask.

"Late!" Mrs. Wilson snapped. "Get up, now, and help Kate fix that order for Miss Tutweiler."

"I don't owe that old biddy anything," Ruby grumbled sleepily.

"No, but you owe those children something," Mrs. Wilson told her.

"What children?"

"Your son. And Kate."

"What are you talking about, Mama?"

Kate could see Mrs. Wilson standing in the hall with her hands on her hips, looking in at Ruby. "You owe them the self-same thing I give you, which is the example of a woman who works hard and keeps her word."

"It's my life!" Ruby's voice was getting louder. "And my choice!"

# Work, Not Fun

Kate slipped into the kitchen so it wouldn't look like she was eavesdropping. But even in the kitchen, she could hear Mrs. Wilson's answer to that.

"Oh, yes, daughter, you have choices. You can stay home and raise your child, or you can get a job, or you can work your pretty painted fingernails to the bone trying to establish yourself in business. But you cannot hang out all night with some no-'count boy and lay up in bed all next day. That's one choice you don't have, not in this house!"

Ruby's reply was sarcastic, but it came from the hall, meaning that at least she had gotten out of bed. "Is the sermon over?"

"I don't intend to repeat myself," Mrs. Wilson told her.

"Good, because I'd like to go to the bathroom."

Kate heard the bathroom door slam. It was pretty obvious that Ruby was mad at her mother for the same reason Kate was mad at Mom. Here they were trying to work hard and earn some money, and they were both getting lectured and bossed around like they were little kids. Kate looked in the fridge. There were still a lot of centers left from the previous batch of candy. Kate got down Mrs. Wilson's *Joy of Cooking* and found the recipe for chocolate coating. It didn't sound too complicated. She found the double boiler pot Ruby had used before and got the chocolate out of the cupboard. She had her finger in the recipe book, trying to figure out what to do next, when Ruby appeared in the doorway.

Ruby was wearing a red silk wrapper, the sort of thing that normally would have made her look like a movie star. But this morning her hair was frowsy and her eyes all puffy.

"Hope you know what you're doing," she said in a nasty voice.

"I don't," Kate said. "But I'm trying."

Ruby turned a burner on under the coffee. "Follow that

recipe, you'll get ordinary chocolate. Mine is something special. It's what they used in that specialty shop where I used to work. It's like what they make in Switzerland." She pushed Kate aside and carefully measured some sugar and cream into the top of the double boiler, then dropped in several squares of chocolate. She set the pot on the stove, adjusted the flame under it, and handed Kate a big spoon. "There. Stir that."

Kate stirred. Ruby poured herself a cup of coffee and sat down. "Reckon I didn't get more than two hours' sleep," she said grumpily.

"Reckon you had a good time," Kate retorted.

"How would *you* know?" Ruby asked.

"Riding motorcycles is supposed to be fun," Kate said, trying to sound equally sarcastic.

"There's more to it than that," Ruby mumbled.

Kate didn't want to seem interested, but she was curious. "You didn't like him?" she asked.

Ruby snorted. "Now what's there to like about a fool like Bubba Lee? All he's got is a fancy motorcycle. And how do you figure he got the money for it anyway, bragging how he doesn't have to work like common folks?"

Ruby came to the stove, took the spoon from Kate's hand, and checked the thickness of the chocolate. "I told him, 'Bubba, I appreciate you taking me around, but don't come by anymore. I got a son to raise and I can see right now you are not the helpful type.'"

"You said that to him? Right out like that?"

Ruby put her hands on her hips and gave Kate a look. "Listen, honey, with men you got to speak up for yourself. Times I didn't, I got in a mess of trouble."

Ruby lifted the hot, bubbling chocolate off the stove and looked at it like it was mud. "I don't know how I got myself into this mess either. Sunday might be a day of rest for some, but looks like we got a lot of work ahead of us. How long till you get out of school for Christmas holidays?"

"Just this week and next," Kate said. "Then I'll be able to help more."

"Good." Ruby gave Kate something that could almost pass for a smile. "I'll be needing all the help I can get."

# 17
# Billy-the-Bad

After the note, the one that said Kate and Ruby ought to finish what they started, Mom didn't mention the candy business again except to ask once or twice if they'd gotten any more orders. Kate figured she had too many other things on her mind. Kate never brought it up either. That's why it was all the way into December before something happened that made things go crazy all over again.

When they'd delivered the first order to Miss Tutweiler, she had ordered six more boxes. If those sold, she told them, she'd double the order just before Christmas or maybe even triple it, because by then people would be looking for last-minute gifts.

They had made Miss Tutweiler's two small deliveries on Saturdays when Kate was home to go to town with Ruby. Both times Kate left a note for her mom saying she was helping Ruby and not mentioning anything about the fact that they were going to town to deliver candy. The second time, it was Kate who delivered the candy, because Ruby didn't like talking to Miss Tutweiler.

Ruby said she'd wait on the bench in front of the ice cream parlor, but when she saw Bubba Lee roar into Ralph's Gas-and-Go, she changed her mind and told Kate she'd wait next door at Brenda's Boutique. Kate was pretty sure she chose Brenda's because it was the sort of place Bubba would never go into.

Kate didn't say so, but she figured it was best for her to deliver the candy by herself. Ruby had a little too much attitude for a person like Miss Tutweiler to handle. When Kate came back from the hotel, she gave the money to Ruby because they had to buy more supplies. Ruby said it would be awhile before they were able to tell just how much profit they were making.

Their first chance to make real money came when Miss Tutweiler ordered twenty boxes. Kate and Ruby worked hard all that week—well, mostly Ruby, with Kate helping out after school—first making the centers, then hand-dipping each piece. The dipped pieces were left to cool on wax paper all over the kitchen.

By Saturday the candy was ready and all they had to do was finish decorating the boxes and fill them. Kate had expected Ruby to be more enthusiastic now that they had finally gotten a big order, but she was moodier than ever. Kate tried to cheer her up by figuring out how much money they'd make. Ruby only grumbled something about how they'd be lucky if they made ten cents an hour. Kate didn't point out that one reason it took so long was because Ruby was very fussy about every little detail—from how an individual piece of chocolate could be touched to the exact place where the bow on the box went and precisely where the fake ruby had to be stuck.

It was late Saturday afternoon when they finally had all twenty boxes filled and looking the way Ruby wanted to look. Mrs. Wilson said they should wait till morning to go to town, but Ruby said she was sick to death of the smell of

# Lost Goat Lane

chocolate and wanted to get it out of the house. She got Mrs. Wilson's big laundry basket and started arranging the boxes. Then she took them out and tried arranging them in a different way. Kate could see the problem. The laundry basket was deep, so the candy boxes had to be stacked one on top of another, which mashed the bows.

Finally Ruby got it loaded and tried to pick it up. She could barely lift it. Kate quickly took the other handle. It wasn't too heavy to carry around the house together, but it was going to be too heavy to lug all the way to town.

Ruby dropped her side of the basket. "Won't work," she said.

"Maybe if we separated them into two smaller baskets—" Kate started to say, but Ruby interrupted.

"It won't work!"

Ruby stomped out onto the back porch. Kate sighed. She knew Ruby wasn't yelling at her. She was just upset because it had been such hard work to make the candy. Now getting it to town was going to be even harder.

"I can ask Mom to drive us in," Kate ventured. "She's already gone to work this afternoon, but tomorrow—"

"No," Ruby snapped. She plopped down on the steps, muttering, "Such a stupid idea."

Kate thought she meant the idea of Mom giving them a ride was stupid, and for a minute she just stood there, not able to speak for feeling so hurt. She didn't want to ask Mom either, but what choice did they have?

"The thing is, Kate, you don't just make a product. You got to get it to market. The more we sell, the more we have to carry. It's three weeks since we started and the only person we're getting orders from is Tutweiler. With just one decent order for her we've got more than we can carry. What if we had others? What if we were actually successful? No way could we lug that much candy to town. And we can't depend on other people, Kate. We just can't."

Kate sat down on the back step next to Ruby. She could see Chip and Luther out in the pasture. They had Billy hitched to the cart and were having trouble getting him to go in the direction they wanted.

"How about using the goat cart?" Kate suggested.

"You out of your mind, girl? Think I'd go peddling the finest chocolates in Florida out of the back of a rattletrap goat cart?"

Kate hadn't looked at it like that. The goat cart was kind of funky, but it wasn't that bad. Anyway, it made her mad that Ruby kept putting down her ideas. At least she was trying.

"Then I'll do it," Kate said.

Kate intended to save what she earned, and if Mom couldn't get together the money to make the mortgage payments, Kate was hoping to help out. But she'd never told Ruby about how they were on the verge of losing the farm, and this was definitely not the time to bring it up.

"Oh, Kate, can't anybody but Daddy make that stubborn old goat go where he doesn't want to go."

"Billy's no more stubborn than our Brahman calves. We got them in out of the hurricane when they were scared and jumping every which way. I can handle Billy."

Ruby didn't answer. Kate got up and walked out to the shed where Mr. Wilson was repairing one of the porch rocking chairs.

"Mr. Wilson, can we use the goat cart to haul our candy to town?"

Mr. Wilson picked up a piece of sandpaper and started smoothing out the new armrest he had just put on the chair.

"Well, you're welcome to try, but Billy's not behaving too well for the boys today." He grinned at Kate. "Course, it might be them more than him. Could be he'll cooperate with you girls. Especially if you coax him with treats."

"I'm pretty sure he'll go for me," Kate said. "Sugar minds me real well most of the time."

Kate went into the kitchen. Mrs. Wilson was fixing potatoes for supper. "Can I have the peelings for Billy?" Kate asked.

"Oh, yes, he loves 'em." Mrs. Wilson smiled. She scooped the peelings into a plastic bowl and handed it to Kate.

The only person who objected to Kate taking Billy was Chip. When she asked to borrow the cart, he said, "No! We're using it."

But Luther handed her the reins. "Take it," he said. "He's being really bad today and won't do anything I tell him. Come on, Chip. Let's go look for turtles."

"Well, okay," Chip agreed. "But just for today," he said to Kate, as if the cart belonged to him instead of Luther.

"Sure," Kate said. "Thanks."

Using potato peels to entice Billy, she led him to the back door.

"That's the idea," Mr. Wilson called out. "Just remember, you can't *make* a goat with Billy's personality do anything. You gotta make him *want* to do it."

Ruby must have seen Kate coming, because by the time Kate got to the back door she was there with the laundry basket full of chocolates, plus some bags of ice to keep them cool. She set the basket in the cart and stomped back into the house.

Kate tugged on the lead rope. Billy followed her a few steps and stopped. She held a potato peeling in front of his nose. He came forward just enough to eat it from her hand, but he wouldn't go any farther until she offered him another, and another, and another. They had only gone a little way down Lost Goat Lane and were still in clear sight of the house, and already he had eaten all of them.

"Come on, Billy. No more treats until we get back."

Billy just stood there. Kate tugged on the lead rope and managed to drag him forward a few steps. The minute she let up on the rope, he backed up. She pulled him forward again. He backed up again. They went forward and back, forward and back. At this rate they'd be here all afternoon.

"You can brace your legs and walk backwards all you want," Kate told Billy. "But either you come with me or you're going to be here the rest of your life, because I am not giving up."

The struggle went on for fifteen minutes. Kate's hand was getting raw from tugging on the rope. She could see Ruby watching from the living room window. Kate was sorry she'd thought of taking Billy, but she wasn't going back to listen to Ruby say "I told you so."

"I'm beginning to hate you," she said to Billy. "You are a really bad goat."

When Kate looked toward the house again, Ruby was walking toward her, looking exasperated.

"Give me that rope," Ruby said in a bossy voice.

Kate hung onto the rope. "We're *not* going back."

"I swear, Kate, you're as stubborn as the goat. Can't you see it's going to take both of us?" Ruby grabbed the rope and gave a powerful tug.

Billy let out a surprised *ba-a-a*, and then, as if he knew he had met his match, he unstiffened his legs and trotted along as if there was nothing in the world he'd rather do than go to town.

"Stupid goat," Ruby muttered.

"He is bad today," Kate agreed, "but I don't think he'll be any trouble once he gets used to it."

Ruby said nothing. Kate could see that she was still upset, probably at the thought of people seeing her beautiful chocolates brought to town in a funky old goat cart.

"We could paint the cart," Kate suggested.

Ruby didn't respond. With a sinking heart Kate realized that once they got rid of this batch of candy she'd never be able to talk Ruby into making more, not if they had to take it to town in the goat cart.

"Please, let's not quit," Kate pleaded.

"Face it, Kate. This is not going to work."

"Ruby," she said, scuffing her ragged sneakers on the road as they walked. "We can't quit. I need the money."

"You need the money?" Ruby laughed in a harsh, unfunny way. Then she looked down at Kate's shabby sneakers and stopped laughing.

Kate waited a minute, then said again, "We could paint the cart."

"With what? Leftover house paint? That's the dumbest—" Ruby stopped so suddenly that Billy was caught off guard and almost stumbled.

"Ba-a-a!" he bleated indignantly, giving Ruby a look like he wished she'd make up her mind whether she wanted to stop or go.

"Oh no!" Ruby exclaimed. "I was so worried about the candy I didn't even think! We can't go like this! Just look at us!"

Kate looked down at her ragged cutoffs and up at Ruby's chocolate-smeared T-shirt.

"I guess we ought to get cleaned up first," Kate admitted, although she hated the thought of going back to the house when it had been so hard to get this far. It was late in the day. She wasn't sure they'd get back before supper time. Mrs. Wilson was right when she said they should wait and go in the morning.

"You know," Kate said, "if we waited till tomorrow, we could paint the cart. You said there was some leftover house paint, and the cart's not that big. It wouldn't take long. Then maybe an hour to dry."

Ruby didn't answer. She stood there for a minute staring hard at something, even though as far as Kate could see, there was nothing in the road. Then Ruby's face lit up like whatever she was seeing in her mind, it was beautiful.

"A white cart," Ruby said slowly. "Trimmed in gold."

"Gold! Where—?" Kate started to ask, but Ruby interrupted in an excited voice.

"Mama's got some gold she uses for making Christmas ornaments. I don't know if it would work. I don't even know how much there is or whether it's the right kind. But can't you see it?" She waved her hand at the goat cart as if presenting Cinderella's coach.

Kate *could* see it. In her mind she pictured the cart, shining white, with "Ruby's Exquisite Handmade Chocolates" painted in the side in gold letters.

"Of course!" Kate shouted. "It's perfect!" Ruby bent down and put her nose close to Billy's nose. "Except for you. You are one bad goat!"

"Not with you, he won't be," Kate promised. "He likes you."

"Ha! This old goat likes food, that's all. He knows I'm the one who brings the table scraps out to him every night."

"Maybe he doesn't want people seeing him looking ordinary either," Kate pointed out. "After all, the only time Mr.

Wilson takes him to town is at fair time. He gets Billy all spiffed up for that."

Ruby laughed. "Is that what you want, you old goat? You want to be spiffed up before you show your horns in public? Okay, Mr. Blue Ribbon Winner, you got it!"

Ruby wheeled Billy around and they headed toward the house. They almost had to run to keep up with him. He was a lot more interested in going toward the house than he had been in going away from it.

"Slow down!" Ruby yelled, laughing.

"Billy-the-Bad," Kate said, trying to catch her breath. "You don't know it yet, but you are about to become Billy-the-Beautiful."

# 18

# Red Velvet

"M y word!" Mrs. Wilson stood with her hands on her hips, surveying the backyard. "Looks like a circus camped back here."

It felt like that, too. There was excitement in the air, the kind you feel when a circus comes to town, especially if you get to slip around back and watch people at work. The cart they'd painted the day before was dry. Kate was now painting the rim of the wheels gold. Ruby sat across from her with a thin brush, lettering the words "Ruby's Exquisite Handmade Chocolates" on the side of the cart.

Mr. Wilson was out in the pasture helping Chip and Luther give Billy a bath. Justin was in the workshop taking the reflector off the old bicycle to use on the back of the cart. When the work was done, they all stood around admiring it. The reflector added the perfect ruby red touch.

"Tomorrow morning," Ruby told Kate, "we'll get all dressed up and blow this town away!" She put her arm around Kate as they walked toward the house. "It's not that dressing up will make our candy taste any better, but it will get people's attention."

Kate could hardly wait till Mom got home so she could tell

her. Mom had barely slid into her chair at the supper table when Kate said, "Oh, Mom, wait till you see the goat cart! It's so beautiful!"

"We washed Billy," Chip added. "With shampoo that smells like flowers. He is the cleanest, whitest goat in the whole world. In the morning Mr. Wilson is going to let us polish his horns and hooves."

"Ruby wanted to line the cart with satin like a candy box," said Kate, "but Mrs. Wilson didn't have any scraps big enough. The red reflector that Justin put on the back adds some color, though. Now the cart's white with gold trim and a ruby—well, a pretend ruby—just like on the boxes of chocolates."

Mom smiled while they talked, but Kate got the feeling that she wasn't really listening, that she had other things on her mind.

"When we go to town Ruby and me are going to wear—"

Mom looked up. "I thought we had this all settled, Kate."

"What?"

"I said you could help Ruby make the candy, but not go to town with her."

Kate's fork stopped in mid-air. "It's for our business, Mom. You said—"

"What I said is, you're not going to town with her," Mom said in a sharp voice. "And that's that."

Mom almost never spoke to any of them in that tone of voice, and then only if they'd done something really bad. Kate felt as if she had been slapped.

She jumped to her feet and ran out the door, slamming it as hard as she could. For a minute she just stood there on the back porch, feeling like her head or her heart or something inside her was going to burst.

She could still hear the voices from the kitchen. "Why, Mom?" Chip asked.

And then Justin asked, "Is it because of the motorcycle?"

"No," Mom said. Her voice was tired. "It's not just because of the motorcycle ride."

"It wouldn't be, I mean—" Justin sounded worried. "It's not because Ruby's black, is it?"

Outside the door, Kate listened for Mom's reply, but heard nothing.

Chip spoke in a shocked voice, "Are you prejudiced, Mom?"

"No, I am not prejudiced!" Mom was almost yelling. "But people will talk. Kate may not care what they say, but I do."

"Say what?" Chip asked.

"What people?" Justin asked.

Kate turned away, not waiting to hear Mom's answer. She went out to the goat shed, where she found Sugar lying on a pile of clean hay. Kate curled up in the hay next to her and thought about running away from home. If Justin could, why couldn't she?

She had been out there quite a while when Mom found her.

"Katie?" Mom's voice was shaky.

Kate didn't answer. Mom knelt down and tried to put her arm around her. Kate jerked away.

"Please listen, Katie. I haven't got anything against Ruby. It's just that there are some people—"

"Who don't like to see black and white people be friends?" Kate interrupted angrily. "I guess you're one of them!"

"That's not fair, Katie," Mom said sadly. "It's just that I've lived in this town all my life. There is still racism. It's not just unpleasant. It can even be dangerous."

"There's laws, Mom! It's not like it used to be!"

Mom shook her head. "Laws don't change the way people feel."

Kate remembered how the guy at the root beer stand had splashed dishwater on her and Ruby when they rode by on the motorcycle. She knew it wasn't an accident. He was probably jealous of Bubba for having so much money and a fancy motorcycle with a pretty girl like Ruby on the back, but Kate knew that wasn't why he'd done it. She remembered the way the guy had sneered, letting her know that he didn't like seeing a white girl having fun with black friends. But so what? She didn't have to be prejudiced just because some lowlife was!

Mom said, "I've never been prejudiced, Katie. And you're right. It's definitely not like it used to be. So maybe I'm wrong to worry about a few—well, to worry about what certain people think or do. But the fact remains that Ruby is not the kind of person—"

Kate jumped up from the hay. "You don't even know her!" she shouted. "You're prejudging Ruby. That's just what prejudice is. Kids at school do it and you do it and everybody does it and you don't even care how it makes people feel!"

"Listen, young lady! I am not prejudiced and I am not a racist! This has nothing to do with Ruby being black. It's just that you are a young girl and she is a grown woman. In case you don't know it, she dropped out of school and ran away—"

"And you're prejudging her for that!" Kate shrieked. "You won't even give her a chance!"

"—and came back and right away started running around with that Bubba Lee—"

"She did not!" Kate shouted. "She wouldn't even talk to him. It was *me* who wanted to ride home on the motorcycle, and we were on our way in the house to make more candy when you showed up. And the things you said and Mrs. Wilson said...Ruby just went off with Bubba that one time because she was so embarrassed."

Sugar got to her feet and stood between Mom and Kate, as if protecting them from each other. "Ba-a-a," she bleated nervously.

"Bah is right," Kate said to Mom in a hard, unforgiving voice. "You prejudged the Wilsons all over the place. That's why you never got to know them. Now you're mad because we did and they're our friends."

Mom collapsed on the hay as if Kate had punched her in the stomach. "Katie, oh Katie," she whispered. "There's so much you don't understand."

Of course. That was what grown-ups always said when they couldn't convince you of something, and you couldn't argue because you didn't know what they were talking about. Kate leaned against the wall of the shed with her arms folded, feeling weak and all yelled-out. Even though she had already fed Sugar at milking time, she put some more grain in her feed box, just to let the goat know that she hadn't been yelling at her.

Mom didn't speak again for a long time, but sat there watching Sugar eat the grain. When she finally did speak, her voice wavered, small and unsure. "What if I drive you girls to town and wait while you deliver the candy?"

Kate sighed. She knew Ruby didn't want to do it that way and she didn't want to do it that way either—not now.

"No, Mom! Don't you see? It's our thing. I had this idea about the goat cart and we've done all this work to fix it up. All we needed was something to line it with and it was going to be so nice! We'd go to town and everybody would love it. We'd be like...like a little one-goat circus. People would laugh and buy our candy and...and now you want to spoil the whole thing!"

Mom had nothing to say to that. Sugar must have decided the fight was over, because she folded her legs and lay back down. Kate flopped down in the hay next to her. She wondered if, when she ran away from home, she'd be able to take Sugar with her.

Finally Mom spoke quietly from somewhere on the other side of Sugar. "Would you like to look in my sewing box and see if there's a scrap big enough to line the cart?"

Kate didn't answer right away. Some fabric to line the cart didn't mean Mom was going to allow her to go to town with Ruby.

"I don't have anything to wear anyway," Kate said, and waited to see how Mom would respond. If she made any suggestions, it would mean she had decided to let Kate go after all.

Mom sighed. "You must have something. Or maybe I do. Come on. Let's take a look."

Mom held out her hand but Kate didn't take it. Instead, she brushed the hay off the seat of her shorts and followed Mom into the house.

When they came into the kitchen Justin was just finishing the dishes, which made Kate feel guilty. This was the second time he had done dishes when it was her turn. It occurred to her that Justin had been a lot more cheerful lately. Maybe it was because Booker had given him some hope, or maybe it was because he was doing better in some of his classes. The last day before Christmas break, she'd heard the boys on the bus teasing him, calling him Einstein because he'd gotten such a good grade on Mr. Jackson's math exam.

"I'll take your turn tomorrow night," Kate said to him as she went by. "And the night after."

Justin looked over his shoulder and grinned. "Good deal," he said.

Kate followed Mom down the hall. Mom's bedroom was small and crowded. Besides the double bed, she had her sewing machine in there and a big cedar chest full of sewing scraps.

Kate didn't go in. She stood in the doorway. If Mom thought she could bribe her with a piece of material for the goat cart, she was wrong.

"What am I going to wear?" Kate asked.

Mom walked over to her closet. She pushed past the dresses she usually wore to church, reached way into the back, and came out with a white skirt. "It'll be a little long on you," Mom said. "But you know how to hem. If you'll hem it and maybe set the button over a little, you can wear it." She tossed the skirt to Kate, then opened the lid of the cedar chest and started taking out pieces of fabric.

Most of them were small, left over from something else. Mom didn't do much sewing now because she didn't have time. But she used to make all sorts of things—dresses for herself and Kate, shirts and shorts for the boys, even swimsuits. When Kate was little, Mom had used the smaller scraps to make clothes for Kate's dolls. Other girls thought it was a big deal if their doll had one extra outfit, but Kate's Christmas doll, no matter what kind it was, always came with an entire wardrobe, everything from cowgirl outfits to party dresses. Of course Kate didn't play with dolls anymore; she had given most of them away. Now Kate hardly noticed the bits of cloth that Mom once would have used to create pretty doll clothes. All Kate wanted now was a piece of fabric big enough to cover the inside of the goat cart.

Not until she got to the bottom of the cedar chest did she find a big piece. It was plain brown. "I guess this'll have to do," Kate muttered. But as she picked up the brown cloth, she saw that it wasn't the last piece. There at the very bottom was a swath of red velvet.

"Ohhh!" Kate dove into the chest after the velvet. "Look at this!"

Mom took the material from her. A dreamy look came into her eyes. "I'd forgotten all about that. I bought it to make myself a Christmas dress two, no, it was three years ago, when I thought Dad was coming back from California." She smiled in a sad way. "He never noticed anything I wore unless it was red."

"Why didn't you use it?" Kate asked, trying to imagine Mom wearing a red velvet dress instead of her usual blue jeans and blue work shirt.

"He didn't come."

"Why not?"

Mom stood there rubbing her hand over and over the fabric. Kate could tell she was remembering Dad.

"I guess he found the life he wanted out there."

"What life?" Kate asked a question that had been on her mind for a long time. "What was wrong with us?"

"It wasn't us. It was—well, your dad always wanted to be a race car mechanic. That was his dream. He had this friend out in California who offered to get him on at the Ontario track. It was just part-time at first, and he was staying with his buddy, so naturally it wouldn't have worked for us to go out there then. Afterwards he got full time work and even got his own pit crew. But they travel, you know, one super speedway to the next."

"He didn't want us along?" Kate asked. She started slowly refolding the scraps and arranging them back in the cedar chest. "Couldn't he at least have come home between races?"

"It wasn't only him," Mom said. "I didn't want that kind of life, traveling from city to city, with my children constantly changing schools. Or a husband who only dropped in now and then."

"Oh," Kate said. In that moment, staring down at bits of fabric left over from clothes Mom had made for them through the years, she knew it was true what Mom had said out in the goat pen, about there being a lot of things she didn't understand.

"Maybe that's another reason the Wilsons and I were never close," Mom said. "They were having a lot of trouble with Ruby there for awhile, and you're right—even though you were little then, I was afraid she'd be a bad influence. I never even asked her to baby-sit for us."

Mom looked down at the red velvet. Her face was kind of pink and she sounded embarrassed. "Later, when your dad left, I figured everybody including the Wilsons were talking, probably blaming me. People around here are pretty hard on divorced women, you know. They may not know why things didn't work out, but they all think they do."

Mom held the red velvet up against her body and looked at her reflection in the mirror. Kate looked at the reflection, too. Mom's long blonde hair had a nice shine to it. Mom would look pretty in a red velvet dress, Kate thought.

"Why don't you make yourself a dress out of it anyhow?" she asked.

"Sure," Mom said bitterly. "The cows would love it." She folded the material and added, "If I was going to make something for myself now, I'd pick a color *I* like."

She dropped the red velvet into Kate's lap. "It's yours," she said.

# 19
# Chip's Revenge

Kate sat in the window seat hemming the white skirt. Since there was no school during this week leading up to Christmas, Justin had gone over to the dairy with Mom to give her a hand. Ruby had asked Kate to keep an eye on Luther while she went Christmas shopping with her parents. Kate could see Luther now, messing around with Chip near the duck pen. Chip was holding a large rusty can. He reached into it and handed Luther what looked like an egg. It wasn't time to gather the eggs, though. And anyway, why hadn't he used the basket? Kate frowned. Why were they playing with the eggs instead of bringing them into the house?

Then Kate remembered that when she had walked past the duck pen yesterday, she had gotten a whiff of a very bad smell. Once, Chip had collected four or five rotten eggs and hidden them in his room. Fortunately Mom had confiscated them before he could smuggle them onto the school bus. Maybe Chip was collecting rotten eggs again, although she couldn't imagine what for. It would serve him right if one broke and the smell got all over him. If that happened Mom wouldn't even let him in the house to bathe. She'd make him wash outside in cold water from the garden hose.

# Chip's Revenge

Kate went back to sewing. And worrying. What if the bank people showed before Christmas and forced them to move out of the house? Where would they go? To an apartment in town? Kate had tried to bring the subject up with Mom. "That's for me to worry about, Kate—not you kids," Mom had said in a sharp voice. "I told you we'll manage!" But if Mom actually believed that, how come she'd looked so unsure?

Justin acted less worried than before; he seemed to think that even if they did move they might not have to change schools. But for Kate, the issue wasn't changing schools. She couldn't see that changing schools would make that much difference. For her, the worry was moving, period.

That was Chip's worry, too. One afternoon when Kate was on her way out to milk Sugar she'd heard Chip in the duck house talking to the ducks, which wasn't that unusual. But this time he was telling them that if any bank people came to get them, he'd help them hide in the tall grass down by the ditch. Kate had actually thought of trying to hide Sugar, but when she mentioned it to Justin he said she was crazy. He said one day the bank guys would show up—maybe when they were at school or before they got up in the morning or even in the middle of the night. They'd have a truck and would start loading things up. He said the bank guys would bring along the sheriff to make sure nobody tried any funny stuff, because it was the law that when you got too far behind on payments everything you had belonged to whoever you owed the money to.

At first Kate thought Justin was just teasing her, but he said it was the truth. That's how she remembered seeing it on TV, too—trucks pulling up at a farm and all the livestock being loaded while the family stood around crying. Kate glanced out the window again, but the boys were gone. The gate to

157

Sugar's pen stood open, and she was gone, too. "Oh, no, not again," Kate muttered. She laid the skirt aside and went to find Sugar.

She called the boys, and then Sugar, but got no answer. Kate walked out to Lost Goat Lane and looked in the direction of the Wilsons', but all she saw was an empty road. She glanced in the other direction. To her surprise, she saw the tail end of Sugar just disappearing down the bank on the other side of the highway. As far as Kate knew, Sugar had never gone anywhere near the highway before.

By the time Kate got to the highway, Sugar was out of sight. At first she couldn't tell which way the goat went. But the minute Kate saw the trail that led through the tall grass, a whole lot of questions were answered at once. Kate knew Sugar had gone down that trail, and she knew exactly why: Sugar was following the boys. Chip and Luther had taken that same trail, the trail that led to the big canal!

Kate didn't have to wonder why the boys went that way. Everything—Chip's disappearances, the grass stains on his T-shirt, the can of rotten eggs—fit together. Why hadn't she figured it out sooner?

She was out of breath when she reached the canal, the part of the canal that circled past the big tree they used to lie under on hot days last summer. Far down the canal she saw Chip and Luther crouched on the bank. Below them lay the alligators, sleeping half-buried in the mud. The alligators were farther from the water than usual, probably because the canal was running so high.

Each boy had an egg in his hand. Before Kate could open her mouth to yell, they flung the eggs. Luther's throw was too hard. His egg sailed past the alligators and hit a tree. Chip's egg landed right in front of the big gator. All of the alligators were awake in a flash. The big one immediately looked in the direction the eggs had come from. Chip and Luther should have run, but they didn't. Instead, they reached into the can for more eggs.

"Stop!" Kate screamed. But Chip and Luther didn't hear her because they were suddenly screaming, too. Then Kate saw what they saw: Sugar, trotting down the bank to the water's edge. The goat waded out into the canal until her fat belly touched the water and then lowered her head to drink.

Chip plunged down the bank toward Sugar just the way he had plunged into the canal to try to save Go-Boy. The two small alligators churned the mud with their short legs, and in seconds splashed into the water and disappeared. Kate was already running, running faster than she had ever run in her life, and knowing, even as she ran, that she was too late.

Up on the bank, the big alligator stood high on his stubby legs, turning his snout first toward Luther, then toward Chip, like he was trying to decide which one to charge. Luther was the closest. Chip, down below, was yelling at Sugar to get out of the water. The yelling must have scared Sugar, because instead of following Chip, she backed away from him, into deeper water.

Kate, running for all she was worth, could hear the big alligator's grunting noise as he swung his head from side to side. Luther took aim and let fly with another duck egg. It hit the alligator right on the head. *Splat!* The rotten insides of the egg ran in yellow rivulets down his big ugly nose and dripped off the end of his top fangs.

Luther dropped the duck-egg can and slid down the bank to help Chip. Both of them grabbed Sugar's collar and pulled for all they were worth. They were dragging her out of the water when the big gator made his move. He hurtled toward them, his mouth wide open.

Kate was just above them. "Chip!" she screamed, and fell,

*woomp!* hard on her stomach. Kate had no breath in her lungs, but she stretched out her arms toward them. Chip grabbed one hand. Luther grabbed the other. They pulled themselves up the slippery bank, dragging Sugar behind them. The big gator slid by just inches behind Sugar's back feet and hit the water with a splash that sent drops up into Kate's eyes. Kate's arms felt as if they were coming out of their sockets, but she didn't let go until both boys and the goat were up on the grass beside her.

For a minute they huddled there, breathing hard. Then Chip got his breath back and started sobbing. "He almost got Sugar."

"Almost got you, too!" Kate was shaking with terror, even though they were now out of danger. She pulled a clump of saw grass and started scraping some of the mud off him.

"Tie your shoes," she said. The laces of his mud-covered sneakers had come undone. While he was tying one, she tied the other. Seeing how little his foot was, and imagining what would've happened if that old gator had gotten hold of it, Kate almost started crying, too. But she was too mad to cry.

"Please don't tell Mom!" Chip begged between sobs that were working their way down to sniffles.

Luther put his hand on her shoulder. "Don't tell my mama either. Please?"

"Of course I'm going to tell!" Kate yelled. "You think I want you to keep sneaking down here till that big gator eats both of you? I'm going to tell and I hope you both get grounded for the rest of your lives!"

Luther's eyes grew wide and Kate could see that he was very scared, either because he thought he might get grounded for life or because it was just sinking in that he or Chip or Sugar or all three of them actually could have been eaten by an alligator.

"I knew alligators were good swimmers," Luther said in a

small voice. "But I didn't know they could move so fast on land. They just lie there in the mud like logs, and their legs are really short. Right, Chip?"

Chip nodded. He was very pale.

"Gators are very fast," Kate said. "They've grabbed people right here in Florida. When a gator sees something splashing in the water, the gator doesn't think, 'There's a dog' or 'There's a boy.' The gator thinks, 'There's lunch!' If you don't want some big gator to think you're lunch, then you better stay away from places where he lives."

Chip looked up at Kate. "But I *had* to," he said stubbornly. "I couldn't let him get away with what he did to Go-Boy." Kate gazed down at his little mud-smeared face. She didn't know whether she wanted to hug him because he was safe or hit him because he had done something so stupid.

"Didn't what happened to Go-Boy teach you anything, Chip? Why do you think Mom didn't want us coming here? And we promised her we wouldn't!"

"We won't come here again," Luther said. "Will we, Chip?"

"No," Chip agreed, "Not till—"

"Never!" Kate shrieked. "You almost got killed. Promise me you will never come here again!"

"Not till we're twenty years old," Chip said. "If you promise not to tell."

"All right," Kate said. "But if you ever come anywhere near this canal again, I swear I will drown you myself."

Chip put his arm around Sugar's neck and looked down the bank toward the canal. There was nothing to see now except still black water with a few eggshells floating on top. "It's okay," he said to the goat. "We ran him off."

"You bet!" Luther said. "I splatted him good!"

"I only got in one throw," Chip said sadly. "Missed him completely."

Luther punched Chip on the shoulder. "Yours landed in front of him. I bet he got a good whiff! And he slid right through it. It smeared all over his belly!" Luther rubbed his own belly gleefully.

"Then he's covered with rotten egg!" A big grin spread across Chip's tear-streaked face. "You know what, Luther? That's a smell that never washes off."

Chip and Luther got to their feet and strutted around as if they had never felt so brave in their entire lives.

I can't believe this, Kate thought. They just about got killed and all they can think of are those stupid rotten eggs!

"Get home, both of you!" she snapped. "And hold on to Sugar's collar so she doesn't walk out in front of traffic on the highway."

Chip and Luther each took hold of Sugar's collar. They walked along beside the goat, their heads tilted together over her neck, whispering. When they reached the highway they stopped.

"Kate," Chip said, "we have a question."

"What?"

"If we got an alligator when it was a baby and never fed it meat," Luther asked, "would it grow up to be a vegetarian?"

"No," said Kate, turning her head so they wouldn't see her smile. "There is absolutely no such thing as a vegetarian alligator."

# 20
# Looking Good

Ruby and Kate wanted to go to town early Saturday morning, but Mom had asked them to wait till she got back from work at noon.

"I'll try to come home a little early," Mom told Kate. "You finish hemming that skirt and when I get here, I'll help you get dressed."

When Mom came in from work Kate was standing in front of the mirror, twirling around in the full skirt.

"Nice hemming job," Mom said, and went down the hall to her room.

Kate followed. "What about a top?"

"Don't you have a shirt that will do?" Mom asked.

"Nothing I can get buttoned anymore," Kate said.

Mom sighed. She stood in front of her dresser for a minute, then, as if making up her mind, opened the bottom drawer and took out a white angora sweater. Kate knew that sweater was Mom's favorite, the nicest piece of clothing she owned. She didn't even wear it to church, but only for special occasions, like to parties back in the days when she and Dad used to go to parties. The only other time Kate could remember her wearing it was the year Kate sang in the sixth-grade Christmas program, and then only because Kate had begged her.

"I guess this'll do," Mom said. She tossed the beautiful sweater to Kate without looking at her.

Kate gave Mom an awkward hug. "If we get our business going," she said, "I'll give what I earn to you. You know, to help make our house payments."

Mom kissed Kate. "That's sweet of you, honey. But I doubt it will make any difference."

If it hadn't been for the soft sweater in her hands, Kate might have cried. If more money wouldn't make any difference, then it must be true that they were going to lose the farm.

I just won't think about it right now, Kate decided, and pulled the sweater over her head. It felt wonderful, and it reminded her of what Ruby had said: it's not how clothes look, but how you feel in them that really matters. She went over to the mirror and took a peek at her new outfit. The sweater was a little big, but that didn't change how good it felt. She whirled around to thank Mom, but the sadness in her eyes stopped her in her tracks.

"Please, Mom," Kate pleaded. "Don't worry about me going to town with Ruby. She really is a good person. She's my friend."

"I know," Mom said, still looking sad. "I understand."

Justin appeared in the doorway. "Ruby's here. She's waiting out by the porch."

Kate and Mom jumped up together. "Let me," Mom said, and moved quickly to the front door.

Ruby was standing by the steps holding Billy's lead rope. She wore a red outfit and she looked, as always, like she'd just finished modeling for a magazine cover.

"Ruby!" Mom called. "Come in here and tell me what you think of Kate's outfit."

Ruby hesitated a second, then handed the lead rope to Justin, who was standing back pretending not to stare but sneaking glances at her when she wasn't looking. Mom held the door open wide, and Ruby walked in.

Kate twirled a circle for her.

"So what do you think, Ruby?" Mom asked. "Will that do?"

Ruby walked around, looking at Kate from all angles. "Nice, but…" With a sudden movement, Ruby unsnapped the red elastic cinch belt she was wearing and fastened it around Kate's waist.

Ruby stepped back, looking pleased. "How's that?"

Mom stared, like Kate had just morphed into a total stranger.

Kate looked from one to the other. "What?" she asked, and headed for the hall mirror.

For the first time since grade school, Kate found herself looking in a mirror and actually liking what she saw. The belt nipped in her waist in a way that made it tiny compared to her hips, which were round under the full skirt. The white sweater, instead of sagging from shoulders to hips, now curved softly over Kate's small but definite breasts.

Mom and Ruby had followed her to the mirror and hovered behind her. "Oh, gosh, do you think…?" Mom began in a doubtful voice.

"Stand up straight," Ruby said, jabbing Kate between the shoulder blades. "You got the same as your mama and me, and it's nothing to hide."

Ruby turned to Mom. "Give that girl another year and she's going to have a terrific figure. Just like yours."

Mom looked embarrassed. "Who, me? I don't—"

Ruby waved at the mirror. "See for yourself, woman. Can't deny what God gave you."

They all stared at themselves in the mirror: Ruby in her red outfit, Kate in a white sweater and skirt, Mom in blue jeans and a blue denim work shirt.

"Red, white, and blue!" Kate laughed. "Look, we're almost the same size!"

It was true. Except for Kate being shorter and a little slimmer, the three of them had almost the same figure.

"You look fine," Ruby said, giving Kate's shoulder a little squeeze. "Just remember, it's not what you hang on your body that matters, it's the body itself. Nothing looks better on a woman than a strong, healthy body."

Mom looked over at Ruby and gave a little nod. Kate saw it in the mirror and wondered if Mom was finally beginning to figure out that even though Ruby was older, she wasn't necessarily a bad person for Kate to hang around with.

Kate twirled away from the mirror and picked up the red velvet lying on Mom's bed. "Look, Ruby. Look what Mom gave us."

"Hey!" Ruby exclaimed. "This is expensive stuff, Mrs. Martin!"

"Let's go see how it looks." Mom took a cardboard box, some thumbtacks, and a hammer, and led the way outside.

Justin sat on the front step holding Billy's rope. Chip and Luther were cartwheeling around the yard.

"See how good we brushed him?" Chip called out.

"And polished his horns, too," Luther pointed out.

"That is certainly one handsome goat!" Mom exclaimed. She walked around the cart to get a better look at the gold lettering on the side. "Who did the calligraphy?"

"Ruby," Kate told her.

"It's beautiful." Mom glanced at Ruby. "Not only artistic, but very professional."

Ruby cut her eyes at Kate in a half-embarrassed but totally

pleased way and lifted out the basket of chocolates so Mom could line the cart with the velvet.

"I was just telling Kate," Mom said, working as she talked, "that if we put this empty cardboard box upside down in the cart and cover it with the velvet, you can arrange the boxes of candy on top. That way it'll look like the cart is full to the brim, and your pretty bows will show over the top."

"Great idea!" Ruby exclaimed. She and Mom began arranging the boxes of candy on the velvet, fluffing up the bows that had been mashed.

"You've definitely got an artistic eye!" Mom exclaimed.

"You, too, Mrs. Martin." Ruby sounded surprised.

The surprise in Ruby's voice caused Kate to wonder if maybe Ruby had prejudged Mom just as much as Mom had prejudged her. Ruby must've thought that because Mom worked at the dairy and wore boots and blue jeans all the time, she was some kind of dumb cowgirl. Ruby didn't know that when Mom had the money to buy fabric and time to sew, she could make the most beautiful and complicated things, not just clothes, but stuffed animals and quilts and wall hangings that were as pretty as any picture.

Watching Mom and Ruby working together, Kate thought that if they'd had a project like this a long time ago, they probably never would've gotten the wrong idea about each other in the first place. At the same time, she was secretly glad that Mom and Ruby hadn't been friends before, because now Ruby was *her* friend.

Billy tugged at the rope, impatient to go. Kate held out two books. "Could we put these in too? I've got to return them to the library."

Ruby tucked the library books down in one corner of the cart and turned to Kate. "There. Are we ready?"

Just then Sugar pranced up and nipped at one of the bows.

"Oh, no you don't!" Mom pulled the goat away from the candy.

"Sugar, what're you doing out again?" Kate demanded.

Ruby said, "Guess she heard there was a convention of beautiful women here this afternoon and figured she ought to join in."

Billy looked at Sugar. "Ba-a-a," he said, tugging on the rope.

Mom laughed. "I think Billy just voted Sugar 'most beautiful female.' As far as he's concerned, the rest of us aren't worth noticing."

Kate smoothed a hand over Sugar's sleek sides, which were getting fatter by the day. "You are definitely looking good," she said to the goat.

"So are you, Katie." Mom smiled at Kate, and then at Ruby. "Go on, you two. Go turn some heads."

"And you!" Mom said to Sugar. "I am going to fix that gate right now so you'll never get it open again!"

# 21

# Downtown

They stopped on the sidewalk in front of the library. Kate dug down under the candy to get the books that were due. A garden club meeting must have just been breaking up, because several women were standing at the top of the steps. The only three she knew were the librarian, a retired history teacher named Mrs. Mayfair, and old Mrs. Bainbridge.

"Will you look at that!" exclaimed Mrs. Mayfair. She came down the steps and scratched Billy between the horns. "Aren't you a darling old thing!"

The librarian read the words on the side of the cart. "Oh, are you selling candy?" she asked Ruby.

"Yes ma'am," Ruby said. "What we have here is for a client, but we'd be glad to take your order."

"Candy, did you say? How much?" asked Mrs. Mayfair.

Kate went inside to put her books on the librarian's desk. When she came out, Mrs. Bainbridge, who was about eighty years old, was hobbling down the steps with her cane. The librarian put her hand on Mrs. Bainbridge's arm to steady her, but Mrs. Bainbridge jerked it away. Even though she tottered, she never allowed anybody except her son Junior to help her. When Mrs. Bainbridge got to the bottom of the steps, she stopped and glared at Ruby. "Are you Ruby?" she asked. She thwacked the lettering on the cart with her cane. "That Ruby?"

"Yes," Ruby said. "I am."

"Don't mind bragging on yourself, do you?" Mrs. Bainbridge said in a cranky voice.

Kate rushed down the steps. "It's the candy we're saying is ex…um…exqui—"

"Just as I suspected. You can't even pronounce it," Mrs. Bainbridge looked down at the word "exquisite" in gold lettering on the side of the cart. "Spelled it right, though." She turned her glare back on Ruby. "You gave my son a box. And he gave you a dollar."

Kate saw Ruby's embarrassed look. Ruby had probably figured out that old Mrs. Bainbridge was the mother of Junior Bainbridge, who ran the gift shop. Kate was sure Ruby hadn't forgotten how he gave them a dollar and told them to "run along."

"That was only a sample," Ruby said sharply. "I told him—"

"Waste of breath," Mrs. Bainbridge interrupted. "Junior wouldn't know good chocolate from a stick of licorice. Luckily, I do. I'll take one. Write it down. One pound for Clair Bainbridge."

"Your address, please?" Ruby asked, pencil poised over her small notebook in a very businesslike manner.

"Everyone knows where I live," Mrs. Bainbridge said haughtily.

Ruby cut a sideways glance at Kate. Kate nodded to let her know it was true; everyone in town knew the huge house where the Bainbridges lived, a house that looked like something out of *Gone with the Wind* and made creaking noises when you went by. But nobody ever said it was haunted, because it was a well-known fact that Mrs. Bainbridge wouldn't tolerate a ghost around the place for one minute.

"So that's one pound, Mrs. Bainbridge?" Ruby asked.

"Yes. Every Saturday."

"Every Saturday?"

"Is there any reason why I shouldn't have fresh chocolates every week?" Mrs. Bainbridge demanded.

"No ma'am," Ruby said, ducking her head and trying not to smile.

Mrs. Bainbridge gave one final glare at the other women gathered around the cart. "Chocolates are good for me," she announced. "They improve my disposition."

The librarian ordered a box of candy and Mrs. Mayfair ordered two. Ruby wrote their names and orders under Mrs. Bainbridge's. Then they led Billy up Main Street to Miss Tutweiler's hotel.

Ruby surprised Kate by saying, "I'll take the order in today. You stay with the cart."

Kate didn't mind waiting outside at all, because people smiled when they saw the cart. Children tugged at their mothers' hands and pointed, and some even crossed the street to get a better look. All the children loved Billy, except one toddler who cried when Billy snatched the cookie out of his hand and ate it in two bites. The little boy's mother didn't see what happened and thought her child was crying because he was scared. She picked him up and kept saying over and over, "There, there, don't be afraid. He's a nice goat. He won't hurt you."

Ruby came out of the hotel with shining eyes. She cracked her purse to show Kate some bills. Kate gasped. For the first time she really had a sense that they were "in business."

As they started back down the street, Kate saw Bubba watching them from the gas station.

"Oh, sweet mama!" Bubba said in a loud voice. "Here she comes."

Ralph laughed. "That gal ain't coming, Bubba. She's going."

Ruby kept walking like she hadn't heard a word they said. Kate covered her mouth to keep from giggling.

Bubba started combing his hair. "Man, what you don't know about women!"

José scooted out from under the car he was working on and sat up. "Bubba, you loco. That pretty thing is not even looking this way."

"The goat looked over this way," Ralph said to Bubba. "Maybe it took a shine to you." He and José laughed.

Bubba revved his motorcycle. Kate saw that he was going to follow them the same way he did before. She hoped he wouldn't come too close. The noise of the bike might upset Billy, who was hard enough to manage as it was.

Just then Mr. Jackson came hurrying up behind them. "Excuse me," he called. "Ruby? Ruby Wilson?"

Kate pulled Billy to a stop. Ruby looked Mr. Jackson up and down, from his short black hair to the books he was carrying under one arm. "Do I know you?" she asked in a cool voice.

"I know him," Kate said. "He's Justin's math teacher."

"I just moved here recently. When school started." He stuck out his hand. "My name's Richard Jackson."

Kate thought Ruby was going to ignore Mr. Jackson's hand, but just then Bubba roared up on his motorcycle. Ruby turned so that her back was to Bubba. She smiled at Mr. Jackson in a friendly way and shook his hand.

"Where are you from, Mr. Jackson?"

Bubba slowed for a second, then revved the engine and roared away. Billy looked after the motorcycle with an evil eye. Kate held tight to his harness until Bubba and his bike were out of sight.

"I'm from Chicago," Mr. Jackson told Ruby. "What about you?"

"I grew up here, but I've been away awhile. Living in New York."

"Bet you're glad to be back," Mr. Jackson said. "This is a great town."

Ruby looked astonished. "You *like* this town?"

Kate noticed that Mr. Jackson was carrying a big bag full of candy boxes. "You bought some of our chocolates!" she exclaimed.

"Well, yes. I did. I just picked them up from Miss Tutweiler. In fact, I'd like to get one more box."

"She doesn't have any more?" Ruby asked in a voice that said she knew Miss Tutweiler did have more.

"She does, yes, but I didn't want to take all of them. She'll be needing some for her other customers. I'd be glad to drive out to your house to pick it up."

"Sure!" Kate said excitedly.

"Well, Kate's my partner. If it's okay with her, I suppose it's okay with me." Ruby smiled at Mr. Jackson in a teasing way and Kate realized that they were talking about more than candy.

"Do you like music?" he asked Ruby. "There's a great jazz group playing in Orlando this weekend."

Ruby looked at Kate. "What do you think, partner? Should I give him my phone number?"

Mr. Jackson reached into his shirt pocket and pulled out one of Ruby's cards, the kind she gave to each of their customers. He flashed it at Kate.

"I already got her phone number. From Miss Tutweiler. I was just asking permission to use it." He arched an eyebrow at Ruby.

Ruby tossed her head, causing the sunshine to sparkle on the beads woven through her tiny braids. "Call if you like, but you're wasting your time."

Ruby took hold of Billy's lead rope and started walking. Kate turned back to wave good-bye. The math teacher was grinning happily.

Kate snuck a peek at Ruby's face. She seemed excited and maybe a little jumpy, but pleased. Kate didn't think Mr. Jackson was wasting his time at all.

# 22

# Betrayal

"Jingle bells, jingle bells, jingle all the way. Oh, what fun it is to ride in a one-goat candy sleigh," Kate sang as she and Ruby walked home from town.

"Dashing through the snow, in a one-goat candy sleigh," Ruby sang. She stopped singing and smiled dreamily. "Just think, if I was in New York right now, I really would be dashing through the snow."

Kate's stomach tightened the way it did when Justin talked about running away. It wasn't what Ruby had said so much as the way she'd said it, like she really wanted to be somewhere besides here.

"Would you rather be in New York, Ruby?"

Ruby walked in silence for a few minutes, and when she spoke, she didn't really answer Kate's question. She said, "First time I left here, it was with a guy. Luther's father. We were just kids ourselves, and oh, did we think we were hot stuff. One thing about New York, it's a reality check on dreams. We got knocked right on our you-know-whats with reality."

"What do you mean?" Kate asked.

"Well, for one thing we found out what it's like to be surrounded by fifteen million people and not one of them care whether you live or die." She paused. "Lots of choices, though. That's one thing cities give you: lots of choices. Problem was, Luther's dad made one choice and I made another, and before you know it, we went our separate ways."

"That's how it was with my mom and dad. He decided to leave and Mom decided to stay," Kate said.

"Yeah, well, it happens," Ruby sighed. "It's easy to get the idea that someplace else is going to be better. But the truth is, no place does you much good unless you can get something going for yourself."

"You have something going here," Kate reminded her. "Maybe more than a candy business. Don't you think Mr. Jackson is cute?"

"Cute? Honey, *I* am cute. *Puppies* are cute," Ruby said. "When I start giving some man the time of day, he better be a whole lot more than cute."

Ruby walked faster, pulled along by Billy. "Slow down, you silly old goat. You took your sweet time going to town and now that we're headed home you're moving so fast we can barely keep up."

"Billy behaved really well, didn't he?"

"Not bad," Ruby agreed as they turned onto Lost Goat Lane. "Not bad at all."

"So when are we taking in the next order?"

Ruby pulled the cart to a stop. Billy struggled to continue toward home. Then he heard Sugar bleating. He changed directions and tried to drag Ruby down the Martins' driveway. Finally Ruby managed to get him to stand still. He pawed the ground restlessly.

"Listen, Kate. There's something I didn't tell you."

"What?" Kate asked, twirling in a circle to make the white skirt flare out.

"We didn't get another order."

Kate stopped twirling and looked at Ruby in disbelief. "We didn't?"

"Miss Tutweiler said people don't buy candy after Christmas."

"What about Valentine's?"

"Yeah, but that's two months from now. Don't you see, Kate? This isn't something that's going to earn us regular money."

"What about Mrs. Bainbridge? She wants a box every week. And Mrs. Mayberry wanted a box and the librarian—"

"Be realistic, Kate. Selling one or two boxes of candy a week isn't a business."

"We just have to find more customers." Kate's eyes brightened. "I know. What about the big gift shops out on the freeway? We could take them some samples."

"And how would we get there?" Ruby asked impatiently.

"Mom could drive us out."

"Kate, I told you before I'm not going to start asking favors from your mom."

"It's not favors," Kate protested. "It's just—it's just being neighborly."

"Oh yeah, like she's really gone out of her way to be neighborly all these years."

Kate stood there feeling as if she'd stepped on two nails at once and didn't know which one hurt most.

"It's just because your parents are older," Kate mumbled. "Because you and Booker were teenagers when we were little kids."

"Or because we're black," Ruby said sarcastically.

"Mom's not prejudiced!" Kate crossed her arms over her chest and gave Ruby a defiant look. "You're the prejudiced one! You think somebody's trash just because they're poor!"

"That's different," Ruby snapped.

"It *feels* the same. If you were rich you never would've asked me to be your partner. You wouldn't even be my friend!" As the words spilled out of her mouth, Kate knew that what she wanted more than anything was for Ruby to say "Sure I'd be your friend, Kate. No matter how rich I was." But that's not what Ruby said. What she said hit Kate hard.

"Well, I'm not rich! And I don't intend to hang around here being poor the rest of my life."

Suddenly Kate realized that this argument wasn't about black and white or about rich and poor. It was about the two of them. Their partnership might not be a real friendship, but it was the best thing she had and she was about to lose it.

"You're going back to New York!" Kate wailed.

Ruby put her hands over her ears. "For heaven's sake, don't screech at me like that! I never said I was going to stay forever!"

"You said we were partners!"

Ruby set her mouth in a hard line. "Look, Kate, I just went along with this goat cart idea because it meant so much to you. But it's kid stuff. We earned ourselves some pocket change, that's all. If you want to keep on doing it, fine. I'll even leave you my recipes. But me, I'm ready to move on. I figure if I can get a business going here, I can get one going anywhere. So why not start where there's more than two customers?"

"All that work!" Kate howled. "Just so you'd have the money to leave!"

Ruby opened her purse and gave Kate a big fake smile. "Well, hold on, girl. You've got some spending money coming, too."

Kate's anger and hurt exploded, so powerful that her whole body seemed to be out of her control.

"Go spend it yourself!" she screamed at Ruby. "In New York!"

# 23
# Christmas Eve

It was Christmas Eve. Kate stood on the porch looking up at the stars, which seemed as cold as she felt. Although she was shivering, she didn't want to go inside. Somehow the chill that penetrated her skin matched the chill she felt in her heart. Even her mind felt numb and hopeless.

Kate could hear the whirr of the sewing machine coming from Mom's bedroom. Mom had been in there with the door shut ever since supper. She was obviously trying to finish a Christmas present for somebody. Justin had gone to bed but Kate knew he wasn't asleep; it was too early. It was just Justin's way of escaping. Mom could pretend this was a normal Christmas, but they all knew. This was the last Christmas they'd ever have here. Then they'd be moving away to some strange place where they'd have no friends. Kate choked back a sob. What difference did it make? She already had no friends.

A noise in the living room caused Kate to turn and look through the window. Chip was pawing through packages under the Christmas tree. Kate went inside. "Mom better not catch you snooping!" she warned.

Chip sat there clutching a bulky package. There were tears in his eyes. "It's soft," he said. "They're all soft."

Kate took the package out of his hands and put it back under the tree. "Don't you want new clothes?" she asked.

"Not for Christmas," Chip sniffled.

Kate led him down the hall to the bedroom he shared with Justin and tucked him in. "It's all Mom can afford, Chip. You know we didn't even get jeans or shoes when school started. We've just got to have new ones. Don't we, Justin?"

"Who cares?" Justin pulled the covers over his head and mumbled, "I hate Christmas."

Kate knew he didn't really hate Christmas. It was his way of saying that no matter what presents they got, it wouldn't make up for what they were about to lose. She felt sorry for Chip, who wanted to find toys, not clothes, under the tree on Christmas morning, and she felt sorry for Justin because she knew he had worked hard to bring his grades up in hopes of making the team. And she felt sorry for herself because nothing, not one single thing, had worked out.

Chip turned his back to Kate and curled up in a little ball. For a few minutes she sat on the side of his bed, patting him on the shoulder and thinking how unfair it was that tonight of all nights the hard truth should be bearing down on them. Chip knew there weren't any toys under the tree. She and Justin knew that if Mom was so broke she couldn't buy toys, it meant she was too broke to make the mortgage payments. They'd be moving for sure, and Justin wasn't going to get a chance to try out for the team. And she, Kate, was not going to be able to contribute anything because she no longer had a way to earn money. She was sort of sorry she hadn't taken the money from Ruby, but at the same time she was glad she hadn't. You don't take things from people who aren't your friends, she thought bitterly, and Ruby certainly hadn't turned out to be a friend.

Kate left the room and tiptoed down the hall. She listened for a minute outside Mom's room. At first it was quiet, then the hum of the sewing machine started up again. She went through the kitchen and out the back door.

When she reached Sugar's pen she stopped and leaned against the fence. She hadn't cried since the day she figured out that Ruby was leaving. Usually a good cry made her feel better but now she felt that it wouldn't make the slightest bit of difference. Whether she cried or not she was going to go on feeling terrible. Tonight, tomorrow, maybe forever.

"Oh, Sugar," Kate sighed. "Mom's going to spend all night sewing clothes and in the morning Chip's going to pout and Justin won't talk and nobody's going to get one single thing they want. It's going to be the awfulest Christmas we ever had."

Sugar bleated softly. Then from the darkness came another bleat, smaller and more high-pitched than the first. Kate shrieked and raced for the house.

When Kate burst into Mom's bedroom, Mom jumped up from the sewing machine and jerked whatever she was sewing behind her so Kate couldn't see it. "What on earth?" she gasped.

"Mom!" Kate said in an excited whisper. "Come quick! Sugar's had her baby!"

Mom's face brightened like a sunrise. She grabbed a flashlight and they ran hand in hand across the yard to the goat pen.

"Shhh," Mom said as she opened the gate. "Sugar wants us to see her new baby, but she'll be nervous and very protective. We don't want to startle the little fellow."

Kate tiptoed to the door of the shed and pushed it open. "Sugar," she said softly. "Hey, Sugar. It's me, Kate."

Mom shone the flashlight beam past Kate. There stood Sugar with two small goats, one golden brown and one black, pressed tight against her side.

"Twins!" Kate exclaimed, going down on her knees.

"Whoa!" Mom said, laughing. "Count again, Katie. I see four more legs on the other side. And they can't belong to Sugar, because they're white."

Kate stuck her head under Sugar's belly to see the third kid. "It's a baby billy!" she exclaimed.

Mom knelt next to Kate, pointing the flashlight beam down so it wouldn't hurt the kids' tender eyes.

"They're so little," Kate breathed. "Barely bigger than rabbits!"

"It's because there are three of them," Mom told her. "With multiple births, the babies tend to be smaller."

While Sugar watched her every move, Kate ran her hands over their silky sides: first the brown baby, then the black one, and then the white one. Each was its own little miracle, a perfect work of art.

"Whose are they?" Kate asked suddenly.

"Why, Sugar belongs to you, Katie. They're yours."

Kate felt a grin break over her face. "Can I give one to Chip and one to Justin?"

By the way Mom hugged her, Kate knew it was a great idea.

"I'll give the black one to Chip, because it's the same color as Go-Boy. Justin can have the white one because it's a little billy." Kate leaned down and kissed the tiniest of the three. "And this little honey-colored one will be mine. She looks like a miniature Sugar. I just know she's going to be the sweetest of all."

# 24
# Goat Christmas

They stayed with the baby goats for almost an hour. Afterwards, it took Kate forever to fall asleep. She heard Mom on the phone and wondered who she would be calling this late at night. Maybe she was letting Mr. Wilson know about the goats. Then the sewing machine started up again but only for a little while. After that, Mom was in the kitchen for what seemed like hours. Kate figured she was making a pie or something for Christmas dinner. She was still rattling around out there when Kate finally fell asleep.

Around four in the morning Kate heard the car pull out. Mom had said she would go to the dairy earlier than usual so she could be home when they woke up on Christmas morning. Kate thought about going out to see the baby goats again, to be sure they weren't a dream. But while she was trying to get up her courage to toss off the warm covers and put her feet down on the cold floor, she fell back asleep.

Then she was dreaming. In her dream she kept hearing the click and clatter of little hooves and the faint tinkle of bells. A shout from the boys' room woke her and she heard the sound of bare feet running down the hall. Kate hit the floor in a single bound. The clicking and jingling continued, and for a few seconds she didn't know if she was still in her dream or awake and running down the hall behind Justin and Chip. The boys screeched to a halt in the doorway of the living room so suddenly that Kate banged into them. No doubt about it now, they were all wide awake.

There in front of them were three small creatures prancing around the room, nosing at gifts under the tree and standing on hind legs to nibble at ornaments.

"Reindeer!" Chip shrieked. "Baby reindeer!"

He made a dive for the nearest one but it leapt away. Justin grabbed for another one but it too sprang out of his reach. Up onto chairs the goats went, around the Christmas tree, under the table, and onto the sofa. For an instant the three little goats paused in a row along the back of the sofa, staring at the children with bright startled eyes. Around each neck jingled a tiny bell—one red, one blue, one green. Then they were off again, leaping across the room, up and over furniture like small kangaroos.

Kate and Mom hugged each other, laughing so hard they could hardly stand up.

"Ma-a-a," bleated the little billy. From outside came an answering "Ba-a-a."

Mom stepped to the front door and opened it. Sugar, looking indignant, marched in, braced her feet on the slippery floor, and called her triplets to her. Sheltered by the Christmas tree and Sugar's warm sides, their wildness vanished. They ducked their heads under Sugar to nurse.

Kate moved close to her own mother and watched in silent wonder.

"Mom," Chip said suddenly, "can we take the baby goats?"

"Take them where?"

Kate said, "He means when we have to move."

Mom looked bewildered. "Who said anything about moving?"

Justin and Kate exchanged glances. It was nice that Mom didn't want to spoil Christmas by talking about losing the farm, but it wasn't really a secret. They'd known for months.

"When the bank takes our place," Justin said.

"What are you talking about?" Mom asked, looking even more confused.

Kate sighed. "We know all about it, Mom. We saw it on TV, banks taking people's farms when they don't have enough money to make the payments, so the animals and families get separated and have to go live somewhere else. Chip's worried about the animals, that's all. He was hoping..." Kate's voice trailed off.

Mom sat down on the couch. For a minute she didn't say a word. The only sounds were those of the baby goats sucking and the tinkle of their bells. Then Mom said in her most serious tone of voice, "Come sit here in front of me, all of you. I want you to listen to me for a minute."

They dropped onto the floor and sat there cross-legged, waiting. Mom looked from one face to another. She didn't smile and they didn't smile. They didn't want to hear what they thought she was going to say.

"I explained this all to you before. I told you we weren't going to lose this place."

Justin shrugged. "Yeah, but you said the bank wouldn't give us an extension."

"That's right," Mom said. "Because in their opinion, a woman with three kids and no husband is not a good risk. Used to be, bankers looked at a person's character. People who had a good reputation for paying their bills didn't have any trouble getting a loan. But now lots of banks don't look at the person. They decide in advance that certain types of people can't be trusted."

"What types?" Kate asked.

"Sometimes women. Or black people, or Latinos. Or people living in certain neighborhoods."

"That's prejudice!" Justin exclaimed. "Can they do that?"

"I was going to help," Kate said, feeling ashamed that she hadn't been able to.

Mom reached out and stroked her hair. "You did help, by not complaining when you had to do without things. And yes, Justin, it is prejudice and it is against the law to refuse to do business with someone just because that person is a woman or a certain race or lives in a certain neighborhood. But some banks, or I should say, some people at some banks, find ways to get around the law. That's what we were up against, and why I made the decision I did."

"What decision?" Chip asked. Kate could tell that Chip wanted Mom to hurry up and get to the point so he could go back to playing with the baby goats.

"The decision that we were not going to lose this farm. If that meant raising our own food and no new school clothes and hardly any Christmas presents—"

"But Sugar had babies!" Chip said excitedly.

"Yes," Mom laughed. "And that's not the only surprise. Here's another one. On Friday, I was able to made one more mortgage payment, so we aren't behind anymore. It was those back payments that brought on all the talk about foreclosure. But now we're caught up." Mom gave them a serious smile. "It'll take most of next year to get the place entirely paid off, but we're through the worst. You kids never should've fretted about losing the farm. I told you I wouldn't let that happen."

Kate thought about the nightmare she had had so often,

even when she wasn't asleep, about how the men from the bank would come one day and they would all have to go nobody-knew-where. Kate didn't know how much she'd been worrying until Mom took the worry away. Already it was starting to get fuzzy and disappear the way bad dreams do after you've been awake awhile.

Justin put his hand on Mom's knee. "Thanks," he said.

"So this place is going to keep on being ours?" Chip asked.

"Yes, son." Mom laughed and hugged him. "It belongs to us and this herd of goats."

Later they opened their presents, which as they'd already guessed were mostly clothes. There were new shoes all around, and two pairs of jeans and two T-shirts each. However, there were a few things they hadn't expected. Mom had made a jacket for Kate and had gotten new book bags for the boys.

Kate had made an extra-large box of chocolates, which she meant to give to the whole family, but now that she had something else for the boys, she gave it all to Mom. And Chip surprised them all with coffee cans full of cookies, which he and Luther had secretly made with Mrs. Wilson's help.

Chip was wrong about all the presents being soft. Justin just hadn't taken his out of hiding and put them under the tree yet. He gave everybody something he had made in woodworking class. For Mom there was a decorative notepad holder to hang on the wall so she could leave them messages. Chip's present looked like a board with holes drilled in each end. Chip stared at it, puzzled, for a few seconds. Then he exclaimed, "I know! It's a swing seat!"

"To replace the one that got munched in the hurricane when the branch snapped off," Justin explained. "I'll help you hang it after breakfast."

Then Kate opened Justin's present for her. She saw right away that it had taken the longest to make. It was a new milking stool, because, Justin said, that time he milked Sugar he noticed that the old one was very wobbly.

"Thank you, thank you," they said to each other as they ripped open each package. But it was hard to focus on clothes or anything else when a baby goat was sticking its velvety nose in your ear or trying to suck your fingers. Then the little black one stood in the middle of a pile of tissue paper and peed.

"Hey!" Chip yelled as he scrambled out of the way. "Watch out!"

"Lucky it peed on wrapping paper and not in somebody's new shoe," Mom laughed. "Kate, maybe you and Justin should put them back in their pen now."

Kate scooped up the white kid and handed it to Justin. "Merry Christmas, Justin. This one's yours."

Then she picked up the black one and nestled it in Chip's arms. "Merry Christmas, Chip. She's yours. You can name her whatever you want."

Chip buried his face in the kid's soft black fur and whispered, "Go-Girl." Then he looked up at Kate and said, "This is the best Christmas present I ever got."

\*\*\*

After breakfast, Justin went out to hang Chip's new swing. Mom asked Kate to help her do a few things in the kitchen, which she did. Then Justin came in and helped. Together it didn't take long. As far as Kate could tell, most of the preparations for Christmas dinner had already been made by Mom during the night. There was a lot of food. It looked like they'd be eating leftovers for a week. Not that it mattered, since it was all stuff they liked and didn't get very often. Finally Mom said that was all until the turkey was done. Kate offered to set the table but Mom said there was no rush, it was early.

"I'm going to take a little nap, then I'll finish up in here," she said, waving them out of the kitchen. "You two go out and help Sugar look after those triplets."

Chip was in the pen with the baby goats. Justin climbed onto the top rail of the fence. Kate climbed up beside him. They sat there together, laughing at the antics of the baby goats. The triplets frolicked about, stopping now and then to look around with startled, quizzical looks that made them seem like cartoon animals come to life. Sugar watched them intently, as if every thing they did was wonderful and amazing.

Around noon Mom came out to see the goats again. The way her eyes sparkled, you would never have guessed that she had been up almost all night. Chip was lying on the ground, letting the baby goats jump over him and sometimes on top of him. Suddenly he leapt to his feet and shouted, "Luther!"

The Wilsons were walking up the driveway. Luther let go of his mother's hand and ran to join Chip in the goat pen.

"Merry Christmas!" Mom called. As she walked out to greet them, she said over her shoulder in a teasing way, "Oh, by the way, Kate, I forgot to tell you. I invited the Wilsons for Christmas dinner."

Kate knew from the way Mom said it that she hadn't forgotten; she'd wanted it to be a surprise. Kate didn't say anything. She didn't know what to say, or even what she felt. Normally Kate would have been overjoyed to see the Wilsons visiting them for a change instead of the other way around. But now she had to face Ruby, and she was not prepared for that.

Mrs. Wilson handed Mom fresh flowers arranged like a centerpiece for the table.

# Lost Goat Lane

"Oh, Mrs. Wilson!" Mom exclaimed. "How beautiful! Flowers this time of year are so special."

"Oh, I wouldn't want to live where I couldn't raise flowers year round," Mrs. Wilson said. "I always got things blooming in my garden."

"We couldn't wait to get down here to see what Sugar brought you all last night." Mr. Wilson grinned, looking over toward the goat pen.

"I'll say," Mom said happily. "Come have a look."

Ruby walked over to where Kate sat on the fence. Kate didn't look at her, but kept watching the baby goats.

"Nice threads you got there, girl." Ruby touched the sleeve of Kate's jacket. "That a Christmas present?"

"Mom made it," Kate said. In fact, it *was* a beautiful jacket, denim patchwork with lace and velvet insets.

"Talented woman, your mom. I wouldn't mind having one like that myself."

Kate knew Ruby was trying to be friendly, but what was the point in being friends with somebody who never wanted to be your friend in the first place and now was about to disappear from your life? Kate focused on the goats, trying to hang on to the good feeling she got from watching them.

Luther was on his knees, nose-to-nose with Go-Girl. "Look into her eyes," Luther said to Chip. "You can see she's very intelligent."

Chip put his face next to Luther's and looked into the little kid's eyes. "Go-Girl," he said softly.

The goat gave a tiny bleat.

Chip turned to Luther. "You're right. She already knows her name."

The sound of a van caused everybody to look toward the road.

190

"By golly," exclaimed Mr. Wilson. "It's my boy!"

"Uncle Booker!" Luther shouted.

"Booker!" everybody shouted. "Hey, Booker!"

Their shouts must have carried all the way out to Lost Goat Lane because the van stopped, backed up, and turned down the Martin driveway. The door of the van swung open. Booker sat there grinning at them.

Mr. Wilson grabbed him by the hand. "Booker, you rascal! Why didn't you tell us you were coming?"

"Look, Uncle Booker," Luther yelled. "Look at our baby goats!"

"Well, if this isn't something! Merry Christmas, Mrs. Martin."

"Good to see you, Booker," Mom said. "You're just in time for Christmas dinner."

"You bet," Booker boomed. "And I'm starving to death. Who wants a ride back to the house?"

"Anybody going down to our house will have to cook for themselves," Mrs. Wilson said. "Mrs. Martin invited us to have Christmas dinner here."

Mom smiled at Booker. "I doubt my cooking can match your mother's, but I promise you won't go away hungry."

"Well, now, I take that as a personal challenge." Booker grinned at Justin. "Just like a woman, isn't it? Always putting us men to the test. Mrs. Martin, if you want to lay one more place, I guarantee it'll get used. Now back off, everybody. Let me get myself disorganized here and I'll be right in."

"Take your time," Mom said. "It'll be a little while before everything's on the table."

Mom and Mrs. Wilson went into the house. Mr. Wilson, Justin, Chip, Luther, and Ruby waited by the van while Booker unfolded his wheelchair, dropped it down beside the van, and lowered himself into it. When he was all settled, Booker glanced over at Justin, who was standing back a little, jiggling his baseball.

"How you doing, Justin? About ready for tryouts?"

"I plan to give it my best," Justin said, standing up straight for a change.

Booker reached into the side pocket of his wheelchair and came out with a worn baseball mitt. "In that case, maybe this'll bring you some luck." He handed it to Justin. "It's the one I played with all through high school and Triple-A."

Kate, still sitting on the corral fence, watched as Justin slipped the glove onto his hand. Justin didn't say a word, just stood there staring at the glove like it was the most wonderful thing he had ever seen in his entire life. With a grin that stretched across his whole face, Justin flipped the ball into the pocket. Booker gave him a thumbs-up sign, then spun his wheelchair around to face Luther and Chip.

"Now what's this I hear about Santa Claus spilling a sleighload of baby goats in the neighborhood? You boys got any proof?"

"Yes, yes!" they shrieked. "Come see!"

Chip tumbled into the corral, picked up Go-Girl, and passed her through the fence to Luther. Luther set her gently in Booker's lap.

"Well, I'll be darned," Booker said. "My old tomcat's bigger than this little tiny thing." He stroked the little goat a minute, then handed it back to Luther. "Better put her back in the pen before her mama thinks she's been *kid*napped." Then Booker turned his chair around and wheeled toward the side yard where Justin was playing catch with Mr. Wilson.

Luther gave the baby goat to Chip and climbed into the corral. Kate looked down at them sitting in the dirt, each with a baby goat in his lap. They talked in low voices, either not noticing or not caring that she could hear them.

"Sugar probably told them how we saved her from that old you-know-what," Luther said.

"You think so?" Chip asked.

"Mama animals do tell their babies things. That's a scientific fact. I'll bet she tells them that story a hundred times."

Ruby came over and stood next to Kate. Kate tried to look cheerful, but the truth was she didn't feel like laughing or smiling. She wished everybody would go into the house, especially Ruby, so she could be alone. Then she heard Ruby take a deep breath.

"You know, Kate, I was thinking maybe we could ask your mom to drive us out to some of those tourist shops along the freeway. See if we could get them interested in our candy."

Kate shot a quick look at Ruby, trying to figure out if she meant what it sounded like she meant.

"Something else I was thinking, just now." Ruby stood for a few seconds staring at Kate's jacket. "I know a whole lot more about clothes than I do about candy. If your mom could teach me to make jackets like that one you're wearing, I know I could sell them. Maybe we could do both."

"We could ask her," Kate began cautiously, trying to hold back the excitement she felt bubbling up.

"You know, we're not going to get any kind of business going overnight. It's going to take at least a year."

"I know," Kate said. In fact, she had known that all along. Just about everything—growing a garden, raising calves up for market, waiting for Sugar's babies to be born, making hand-dipped chocolates—everything took a long time, and usually a lot longer than you thought it would.

Ruby looked off into the distance. "Thing is, Kate, I've

never stuck to anything for a whole year. Not even high school."

Kate felt the determination she always felt when somebody acted like something wasn't possible. She said, "I'm good at sticking to things. No matter how long it takes."

"Think you can stick to this?" Ruby asked.

"Think *you* can?" Kate shot back.

"I'm willing to try."

Kate felt like jumping for joy, but you can't very well jump around on the shaky top rail of a fence. She started climbing down. As her foot touched the ground, she thought of something else. She turned to face Ruby. This wasn't the best time to ask, but she had to know.

"Ruby," she asked, "do you still think people like us are 'white trash'?"

Ruby looked down at her beautiful silver-colored fingernails. Kate could see that she was embarrassed. Then she shrugged and said, "So I made a mistake." She reached out and rubbed a velvet patch on the sleeve of Kate's jacket. "But it didn't take me all that long to change my mind about you, did it?"

"I guess not."

Ruby gave Kate a funny little sideways smile. "So how long is it going to take you to make up your mind about me?"

Kate didn't answer. She just put her arms around Ruby and hugged her, hard. Ruby's arms circled her shoulders, hugging back. "Come on, partner," she said, "let's go in and help our moms get dinner on the table."

"You go ahead," Kate said. "I'll be along in a bit."

She needed a few minutes alone to sort out things in her head. Or maybe in her heart. She wasn't sure which.

Ruby gave Kate's shoulder a squeeze and went into the house. Kate leaned against the fence and watched Mr. Wilson and Justin over in the side yard playing catch with Booker. Then they headed toward the house.

When they got to the porch, Booker turned his wheelchair backwards so Justin and Mr. Wilson could lift it up the steps, because their house didn't have a ramp like the Wilsons'. Then Booker seemed to change his mind. He said something, and Mr. Wilson went on inside. Justin moved away from the house and started pitching the baseball in the air. Booker wheeled himself toward Kate.

"Looks like you're thinking some mighty heavy thoughts for a Christmas Day," Booker said. "Everything okay?"

Kate smiled. "Better than okay...I think." Her smiled faltered a little, because the truth was, she was only hoping everything was okay. She wasn't totally sure.

"Some little thing gnawing at your mind?"

That's when it occurred to Kate that maybe Booker could help explain something she couldn't get straight in her head.

"I was thinking about how people prejudge other people. That's the same as prejudice, right?"

He looked hard at Kate. "You worried about somebody around here being prejudiced?"

"Not exactly." Kate hugged her new jacket close to her chest. "Just wondering how you keep from having ideas about somebody when you first meet them. And if you do have ideas, like you think this person is, well, something you don't like, is that prejudice?"

"Could be," Booker agreed.

"But you can't help thinking *something*," Kate pointed out. "Does that mean everybody's prejudiced?"

Booker, Kate had noticed, never stayed still very long. He sat pretty still while she was talking, but as soon as she finished, he started rolling his chair around in a tight circle, practically doing wheelies with it. When he stopped, he was facing

away from her, toward Justin, who was out in the yard playing catch with himself.

"Come here, Kate," Booker said suddenly.

Kate went to stand by him.

"Let's say I'm a coach and you're a coach. There's that boy
we're watching out there who wants to play on our team. But
he doesn't look like much of an athlete from here, does he?"

Kate frowned, but she nodded, because what Booker said
was true. Justin was so skinny that if you didn't know him,
you wouldn't know how good a ball player he was.

Booker glanced up at her. "So we're agreed? From an ath-
letic point of view, he doesn't make a very good impression."

"Not at first," Kate admitted.

"Which means we've prejudged the boy. Now let's say he
walks over and asks for a chance to try out. Me, I got my mind
made up. I say, 'No, son, I already decided you don't have
what it takes.'"

Booker grinned up at Kate. "But you, Miss Coach, you say,
'Well, boy, I'm going to give you a chance to show me how
well you can handle a ball.' When he does that and you see
he's a good player, you put him on the team."

"Yeah," Kate said, relieved that Booker had worked out a
scenario where Justin made the team.

"The problem wasn't the prejudging, because like you say,
everybody probably does a little prejudging, even when
they're not meaning to. It was not giving the boy a chance,
that's what made one coach what you'd call prejudiced. But
the other coach, she did give the boy a chance, and when she
saw she was wrong, she right away changed her mind."

"Oh." Kate remembered the first day she and Ruby took
candy to town, how Ruby had called the townspeople close-
minded because it looked like they weren't going to give their

candy a chance. But they had. Even Miss Tutweiler had been open-minded enough to try it.

"So prejudice is not prejudging? It's being close-minded?"

"I'd say that's about right," Booker agreed.

He glanced over at the goat pen. Luther was looking at his new watch. He waved his watch arm at Chip. As if that was a secret signal for lunch, the triplets suddenly leapt away from the boys, stuck their heads under Sugar's belly, and started nursing.

Booker looked at Kate. "Did you see that?"

"What?"

"Those kids think it's lunchtime. The smells coming out of your mama's kitchen got me thinking the same thing. You reckon if we went in she'd give us a nibble of something?"

Kate laughed. "Sure! I already made cheese dip for crackers and raw vegetables."

"Exactly what I had in mind," Booker said, and yelled, "Hey, Justin!"

Justin turned, grinning. Then he tossed the ball straight up. Kate watched it sail up into the blue sky. It seemed to her like only pure happiness could make it go that high.

Booker gave a long whistle, then wheeled himself toward the back door, calling to Luther and Chip as he passed the corral, "Hey, men. Give us some muscle here."

Together, Kate, Justin, Chip, and Luther hoisted Booker's wheelchair up the three steps to the back porch. Just as they pushed through the screen door, somebody in the kitchen must've told a joke, because Kate heard Mom, Ruby, and the Wilsons burst out laughing. She looked at Justin, who was grinning. He was probably thinking the same thing she was: that Christmastime or anytime, it couldn't get better than this.